Wagon Train

Based on the television series
starring Ward Bond and Robert Horton

By
TROY NESBIT

Illustrated by
JOHN USHLER

WILDSIDE PRESS

Diamonds! The word blazed through camp like a prairie fire, driving every other thought from men's heads. They had started west to get rich, and here was their chance, before reaching the end of the journey!

Young Danny Green was as anxious as anyone to find a diamond mine. But Major Adams, head of the wagon train, had strong doubts about a diamond field in the Rockies, even when he saw the diamonds with his own eyes.

"You'd rather be rich than alive!" he roared at the sullen wagoners. "If we don't move, the Utes will have our scalps!"

Before the trip was over, Danny had reason to wish they had listened to the major. With Flint McCullough, scout for the wagon train, the Gower twins, and Caleb the crow, the boy followed a deadly trail of lies, robbery, kidnapping, and attempted murder. At its end he found the biggest "treasure" a boy could want—the assurance that Major Adams and Flint McCullough felt proud and lucky to have him in their wagon train.

CONTENTS

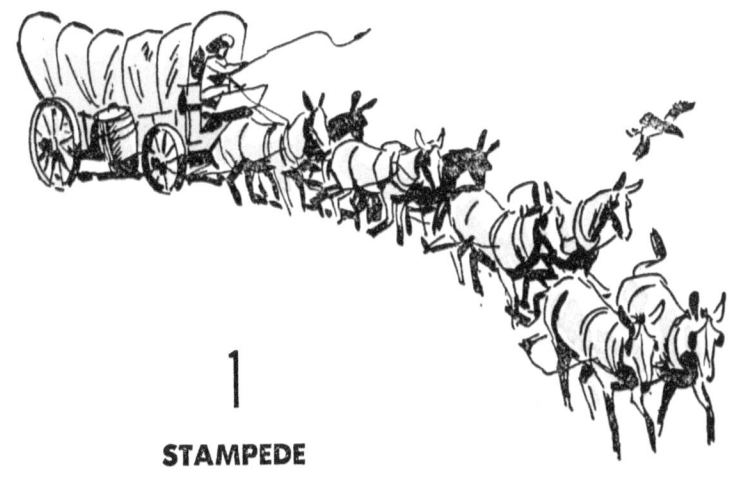

1

STAMPEDE

With every clap of thunder Danny Green felt the mules jerk nervously at the reins. Each new lightning flash drove the animals closer and closer to panic. The first drops of rain hadn't fallen yet, but an ugly green-black cloud tossed and tumbled across the wagon trail ahead. In a matter of minutes it would be dropping tons of water straight down on the mules. Then, Danny knew, they would really give him a hard time.

Sudden angry outbursts from drivers in front and behind and on either side told Danny that he wasn't the only one in the wagon train who was having trouble. Grown men also had their hands full with jittery teams. There was confusion everywhere. And no wonder!

This was no ordinary August storm approaching. The ominous clouds seethed like a volcano. Danny stood up on the seat of his rumbling Conestoga wagon and looked back over its dirty white canvas top.

Behind him rose the same frightening wall of cloud!

The wagon train was in the center of a storm the likes of which Danny hadn't seen in the five weeks and more he had been driving the wagon west from Independence.

Thunder roared like a thousand bass drums, and the lead mules reared. At the same moment a big black bird appeared above their heads, as if it had been catapulted upward into the air. And, indeed, it almost literally had been. The bird was a crow that had been riding perched on the collar of one of the lead mules. Now it struggled futilely against the rising wind for a few seconds, then dived for shelter straight through the small round opening in the canvas wagon top behind Danny's head. To the sound of the wind, the bird added its own raucous shrieks: "Hi, Danny! Hi, Danny! Hi, Danny!" There were times, the boy thought impatiently, when he wished he had never taught the bird to say a single word.

"Shut up, Caleb!" he grumbled. "I'm busy."

The mules reared again.

"Whoah! Whoah! Take it easy!" Danny tried to keep a soothing voice while he yelled against the wind at the same time, but he could scarcely hear himself now. Certainly the mules couldn't hear.

Rain in a sudden pelting sheet dropped out of the sky, and the eight-horse team directly ahead veered sharp left. The wagon they were hauling tilted up, paused crazily on two wheels, then fell over on its side. As if by magic, another team appeared out of nowhere, pulling up so close on the right that the animals shouldered Danny's mules, and the wagons almost locked wheels. Danny's team, eyes wide with new fright, strained forward with all their wiry strength. They broke into a dead run, hauling the huge wagon as if it were nothing more than a buggy.

Danny marveled. How could the creatures do it? This wagon weighed at least four tons with its cargo of heavy paper, metal type, and a complete printing press.

The wind carried off Danny's broad-brimmed hat and

almost ripped him from the wagon seat. Then came a new torment. Hailstones as big as walnuts drummed painfully through the boy's shock of thick, curly hair. The sudden hail battered the mules, hammered the animals' sensitive muzzles, bruised their eyes and ears—and drove them completely, wildly out of control, each seeking to escape the aching terror in a different direction. Then, all at once, a devilish harmony united their efforts. Their long legs strained in unison, and they heaved the great Conestoga out of its ruts and raced with it at right angles to the four files of wagons in the train.

In that direction, Danny knew, lay disaster. A deep gully slashed through the prairie only a little way off. His powerful hands locked like vises on the reins. He braced himself on the heaving seat and pulled back with all his might. Fear doubled his strength. Released from some-where came the power he needed to regain control of his eight mules, and he managed to turn them. Out of the tail of his eye he caught a glimpse of what he had escaped —a brown, surging, murderous flood that filled the gully only a few yards away.

Now at last the mules began to tire. The cloudburst had changed the dry clay of this sagebrush country into mud as slippery as grease, and the animals' hoofs slid every which way. One of them lost its footing completely and fell. Another went down. The remaining six dragged their fallen mates a little way—and then it happened! The wagon skidded sideways. A front wheel caught on a deeply rooted shrub, and the axle snapped. The wagon bed dropped, plowed into the earth, and the wild race came to an abrupt and violent end.

Danny pitched forward. Although the fall knocked all the breath and most of the wits out of him, he had just enough sense to roll quickly away from the mules' flailing hoofs.

What he did next, Danny never quite knew, but there came a moment when he realized he was standing with a firm grip on the lead mules, while they and their mates gradually calmed down. They were spent—too exhausted for another outburst of panic. They merely stood with heads hanging low, the very picture of listless dejection.

The frenzy of the storm, too, was passing. The whole

violent explosion of wind and rain and hail ended almost as suddenly as it had begun. In the full brilliance of the midday August sun, Danny surveyed the wagon train. As a rule it traveled in four parallel lines of ten wagons each. But no lines of any kind were apparent now. The outfits were scattered in every direction, here where low ridges began to rise out of the prairie. Away to the rear he saw the wagon that usually moved along ahead of all the other prairie schooners like a flagship at the head of a fleet. Somebody had given her a flagship name too. *Santa Maria* was painted on her side, and she belonged to the Columbus of this expedition—the wagon train's master, Major Seth Adams.

The major himself was galloping on his bay horse from one wagon to another, as if to survey his scattered flotilla, and Danny knew that the big, fatherly man was giving out his own particular brand of encouragement. Sure enough, he had some of it ready when he approached Danny. "Cheer up, my boy. This is the way life is—short and full of blisters. Are you all right?"

"I guess so," Danny answered without much conviction.

"But look at what happened there." He pointed to the broken axle.

The major whistled. "Busted all to flinderjibs, ain't she! Too bad the rain didn't last a little longer. It would have saved you a lot of trouble."

"How do you figure that?" Danny half-guessed what the major was going to say.

"Water would have been high enough to float that misbegotten ark of yours up over the snag she got caught on."

Danny smiled. The major was always joshing him about the big blue Conestoga wagon that did have sloping ends, a little like a boat.

"You got a spare axle?"

"I did have one," Danny answered. "But I let Asa Gower have it when the *Hunkidori* broke down this side of Bent's Fort. Can you find me another? I'll need someone to give me a hand with it too."

"Very well, sir," the big wagon master said, saluting. "Right away, sir." This was part of a game he sometimes played with Danny who was the youngest driver in the train—barely fifteen and strong, though he didn't look it because of his slightly stooped shoulders and thin face. The major was old enough to be his father, but it amused him to pretend that young Danny bossed him around. Some said it was because he had no son of his own and wished he did have.

"I ought to be able to catch up with the train tomorrow," Danny said. Then he had a sudden limp feeling in the pit of his stomach. He wasn't sure he wanted to stay here alone tonight, even if he did have a man from one of the other wagons to keep him company. Everybody knew they were getting close to Indian country, and only last year the Utes had swooped down out of the mountains that Danny could see not far ahead. The warriors had done plenty of damage around the settlement called Trinidad somewhere fairly close by. So far on this trip nobody had actually seen an Indian. But if Danny was going to encounter hostile Utes, he would rather do so when he was with the train, not half a day behind it.

"This train is sticking together!" Major Adams barked, relieving Danny's worry on that score. "Nobody will move from here until you're ready. I'll tell Flint to dig up another axle someplace and round up some men to lend a hand. Now get your tools out. God helps them that helps themselves."

Danny opened the toolbox on the side of his wagon. As he readied the jack, he hoped Flint would remember to bring another one. Raising the wagon to install the new axle would be a considerable job. The cargo was heavy, and some of the big bundles of paper in it had probably shifted forward when the broken axle plunged into the ground.

Danny hadn't had any choice about the way in which the cargo was stowed, because the loading had been finished when he was hired to drive the wagon. A complete print shop had been packed into the big Conestoga by a man named Valentine Cluggage—Colonel Valentine Cluggage —who had bought it cheap and was shipping it to Santa Fe.

Danny smiled at the thought of the excitement he had felt when the elegant colonel offered him the job of driving the press west, and of operating it once they got it to Santa Fe. The whole thing had seemed too good to be true. Danny had been thinking for a long time that he would like to go West. He had started to learn the printing trade in

Independence before his father and mother died of small-pox, and the shop had been the only home he had known for the last three years. It took something big and surprising like the colonel's proposal to shake him loose. So here he was more than two-thirds of the way to dreamed-of Santa Fe, and as soon as he got the broken axle fixed, he would be on the trail again.

The *plop-suck plop-suck* of hoofs in mud told him that help for the wagon was almost here. The major himself led a little group of men who were bringing tools and a spare axle.

"Flint," the major said to a compact, neatly built young fellow who rode a sorrel mare, "you can see why Danny calls his wagon the *Poor Richard*. She sure looks poorly, don't she?" Then, laughing at his own joke, the major rode off and left Flint in charge.

"You know, Danny," Flint said, pushing his hair out of his eyes, for he, too, had lost his hat in the storm, "I've been meaning to ask you for the longest time. Why do you call it the *Poor Richard?*"

"I thought everybody would know that. It's a print-shop

wagon, and Benjamin Franklin—you've heard of him—used to be a famous printer, and he called himself Poor Richard. So that's all there is to it."

"All right, let's see what we can do here," Flint said, and he began directing the men, most of whom were older than his twenty-seven years. Soon there came a creaking and groaning from the big wagon bed, as they turned jacks under the front end of it and slowly lifted it out of the mud. The motion of the wagon and all the stir of men and horses seemed to suggest to the crow that it was time to take an interest in what was going on.

"Hi, Danny! Hi, Danny! Hi, Danny!" Caleb screamed and emerged from the wagon. At intervals all through the repair job he repeated the companionable greeting that Danny had taught him in the lonely print shop back in Independence.

Finally the men shoved the big wheels into place and "doped" the hubs, packing the grease in well to keep them from screeching and getting hot.

"Son, you're ready to roll," Flint said at last.

But to Danny's surprise the other wagons were not preparing to move on. Instead they were circling up as they always did when they made camp for the night.

"It doesn't look as if anybody's rolling any farther today," Danny said. "What's the idea?"

"We've been held up so long that we couldn't get to a camping place that's any better," Flint answered. "And you never can tell what one of these cloudbursts is going to do. It may have washed a deep gully across the trail so that we'll have to go several miles out of our way. I'll do a little scouting this afternoon so we'll know what we're up against before we start tomorrow morning."

The teams of eight or ten mules and horses were being unhitched. Drivers were placing strong rawhide hobbles on the feet of the animals. Half a dozen fires, built with emergency kindling supplies, were spluttering to life outside the circle of wagons.

"Is there anything the major isn't prepared for?" Danny wondered. More dry firewood came out of hiding, and cooks got the water they needed from the kegs each wagon carried.

Danny hurried to close the circle by adding his own

wagon to it, then he hobbled his mules and joined the group around the major's cook-fire where he ate his meals. Here he heard talk of something he had missed while he was helping to repair his wagon. He listened carefully as he ate.

A lone rider, it seemed, had appeared from the east, chatted for a while with Major Adams, then moved on toward the west and higher country. And now, Danny could see, the wagon master was in a bad mood.

"What makes *him* so full of wrath and cabbage?" Danny said to Flint in a low voice.

"I don't know. Why don't you ask him?"

Danny asked, and he got an explosion.

"Did you see that low-down, cross-eyed son of a stuffed baboon that rode through here a while ago? Well, he's the captain of the wagon train that has been trying to get ahead of us ever since we left Independence. Today he's done that very thing."

"How did he do it?" Danny asked. He had seen no train pass by.

"He made a fool out of me as easy as shooting. To begin

with, that freak hailstorm missed him altogether. He could travel while we were having our stampede—and fixing your wagon!" The major looked ferociously at Danny. "See that ridge over there? That sneaky polecat had his train go along behind the ridge, while he came over and talked to me so sweet and sympathetic about all the trouble I was having. Look!"

Danny stared up the long, gentle slope. There, outlined against the mountains in the distance, were the white tops of wagons.

"I swore I'd never let him get ahead of me," the major went on, "but now we have to poke along behind him all the way up over Raton Pass and all the way down the other side."

"Why so?" Danny asked.

"Because we see the last of flat country, starting just a little way from here. Then the wagons will have to travel single file, not four abreast. We couldn't pass him, even if we caught up with him. There are places where he *couldn't* let us pass even if he wanted to—which he doesn't. He's made up his mind to get his cargo into Santa Fe ahead of mine, so he can ask a better price for it."

A call from the other side of the circle put an end to the major's tirade. "Stagecoach! Stagecoach!" The word swept through camp.

Danny felt a quick thrill of anticipation. For days now he had felt the same way, every time the stagecoach came from the east and passed them on the trail. He was expecting his employer, Colonel Cluggage, who had stayed behind, tending to some business in Independence. The colonel had promised to overtake the train before it reached Raton Pass, and Danny would certainly be relieved to hand him responsibility for the wagon before they entered mountain country.

But it soon became clear that this stagecoach did not have Colonel Cluggage aboard—for the very good reason that it didn't come from the east. Danny had to look toward the mountains and shade his eyes against the brilliant afternoon sun before he saw the high, swaying vehicle that was rushing toward the circled wagons.

"Ah-whooh-wah!" The familiar yell of the driver announced the approach of the stage. And Caleb, who waddled about camp, echoed with a bloodcurdling "Ah-whooh-wah!" which gave Danny the creeps because every-one said that it sounded just exactly like an Indian war whoop.

The stage driver reined in and came to a full stop near the major's fire. "I hear you're in serious trouble, sir," he said, looking like an emperor on a high throne, a patroniz-ing emperor.

Major Adams let out a bellow of pure rage. "I'll be dogged if you don't turn me into a curly wolf and make me want to howl! I suppose you heard that fairy tale from a good-for-nothing wagon train captain just ahead of us? You can see for yourself he's a liar!" Then the major pulled himself together and asked, "Anything new in Santa Fe?"

"About the same as always, except we had a mighty nice little robbery the day before I left."

"Stagecoach?"

"No. Some fellow broke into a rich Mexican rancher's place and made off with a lot of gold and jewels and stuff."

"Catch him yet?"

"No, they don't even know who he is or what he looks

like. Could be I've got him right here in my coach, helping him make his getaway."

A shiver of excitement stirred the back of Danny's neck under his long hair. The driver was only joking, about the getaway, at least. But just the same, this came close to being the kind of thing Danny had dreamed about sometimes back in the print shop in Independence when he was running off a handbill that offered a reward for the capture alive or dead of some road agent who had held up a stagecoach.

The driver's second bit of news created more of a shiver in the train. There was Ute Indian trouble a-brewing, he said, and the major had better keep a sharp lookout. Hundreds of Utes seemed to be gathering west of Raton Pass in the mountains somewhere.

"Nobody's sure what they're up to, but no good, if you ask me. Better double your guard." With that the driver gave a great flourish of his long whip. The cracker on its tip sounded out like a gunshot, and the eight beautiful horses lunged eastward. The creaking red coach was soon out of sight.

A robber—and Indians—ahead!

There was no doubt that Major Adams took the stage driver's warning about Indians seriously. That night he did double the guard.

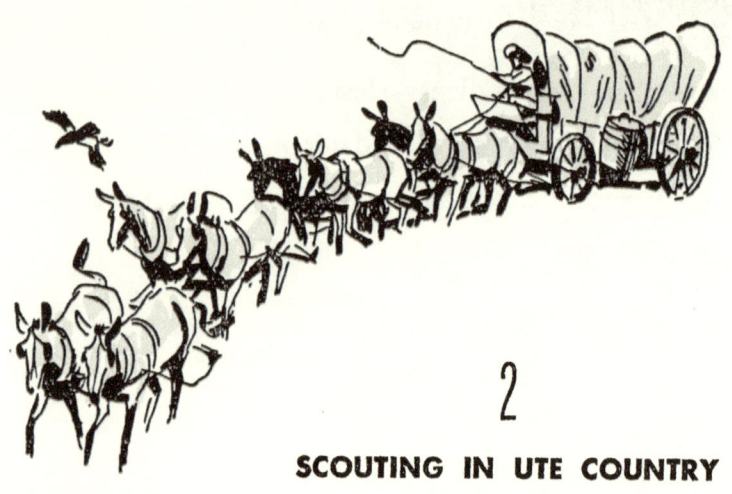

2

SCOUTING IN UTE COUNTRY

The sharp crack of a revolver shot woke Danny. He threw back his buffalo-robe cover and opened his eyes.

What—who—Utes? At the thought of an Indian attack, he grabbed for his rifle. Should he stay here under the wagon where he would have some protection? Or should he scramble out and wait for orders?

"Wake, snake! Day's a-breakin'!" croaked a voice in his ear.

Danny drew himself up on one elbow and glared at Caleb, perched on the new axle above his head. "So that's all it is!" The revolver shot at four in the morning always signaled the start of a new day, and he had taught Caleb to respond to it with the nonsense greeting that he repeated over and over: "Wake, snake—wake, snake!"

The next moment there came a groan from under the nearest wagon. "Ooh! Aah! It's so 'nation cold my joints are stiff," said a man known to Danny only as Jack the Jug. Jack had been hired as a driver at the last moment, and he was never long separated from a whisky bottle, of which he seemed to have an ample supply.

Danny rolled out from under the wagon, heaved his buffalo robe onto the seat, and surveyed with relish the busy, noisy circle of wagons. Pans rattled; harness chains jangled and chimed; horses snorted and stamped. Occasionally a mule uttered its own peculiar cry to the fast-disappearing night. Here was bustle of a kind that Danny never seemed to get enough of. He looked forward to breakfast too, although it was always the same old thing—bacon, beans, and coffee.

As he ate near the fire this morning, more than one man stopped to ask him if he thought Colonel Cluggage would catch up today. Like the colonel, these were businessmen who thought that Santa Fe would offer them opportunities for investment or new enterprises now that the effects of the Civil War were wearing off and railroads were bound to cross the continent soon.

To all of them Danny replied, "I don't know, but I surely hope he comes in time to help with the mountain driving."

The drivers of all forty wagons had their outfits lined up on the trail two hours later. Major Adams made a last-minute inspection of the train that had been so badly buffeted yesterday in the storm.

"How's that front axle of yours?" he asked Danny.

"Seems fine. Thanks for getting the men to help me out. I'm certainly glad it got fixed before the colonel caught up with us."

"Son, that little mind of yours is all cluttered up with big trouble," the major said. "Nothing bad has happened to you yet. Wait till your wagon rolls off a cliff tomorrow or next day." Then he added seriously, "Stop worrying, Danny. You do as good a job of driving as any of these brass-throated mule skinners."

Danny smiled, a little embarrassed. It was something special to get praise from Major Adams, who seemed to spend a good deal of his time grumbling. "Well, I won't mind when the colonel does catch up. When he hired me in Independence, I didn't think I'd have to drive every inch of the way from there to the Rockies."

"You didn't?" The major sounded a little surprised.

"It was this way," Danny explained. "He hired me mainly to work in the print shop that he's going to set up in Santa Fe. But I've handled mules, and I said I would do some of the driving. The trip is two-thirds over, and he hasn't driven a bit."

"Chances are he'll be on the coach that will catch up with us today. Then we'll see how good he is at easing these knot-headed mules around some of the bends on the trail over the pass. He'd better be good. There's one place where a wagon can fall two hundred feet—straight down!"

The major rode off. A minute later he bellowed as he took his place at the head of the line, "All's set!"

Danny's eyes checked over the harness on his team and waited for the final order.

"Stretch out!" the major shouted. "Wagons ho!"

"Hep!" yelled the forty drivers, and their whips cracked

in the cool morning air like gunshots.

With a groan and creak and rattle and rumble the caravan headed off toward the foothills that rose up ahead. The sun was well over the horizon now, and it brought out in sharp relief small details of the prairie which the wagon train was leaving behind. Danny couldn't be sure, but when he looked back once he thought he saw something moving in the distance. As the trail climbed, he looked back again and again. Something *was* approaching rapidly.

"Hey, Flint! Is that the stagecoach?" Danny called when the scout rode by.

"Sure it is."

"If Colonel Cluggage is on it, may I ride with you today?" Danny asked.

"Of course you can, if the colonel will drive the wagon."

Danny cracked his whip impatiently. All the way across the prairie he had envied Flint McCullough his freedom to ride out ahead of the wagons, looking for buffalo, for camp sites—for Indians. Riding a good horse was something that Danny dearly loved, and the colonel had sent three fine geldings along in the cavvyard, which was the

herd of extra horses and mules that accompanied the train to provide mounts for the men and replacements for injured or exhausted pull animals. As soon as Danny could turn the reins over to someone else, he would spend his time riding the colonel's horses. He had visions of himself, day after day, up ahead with Flint, at liberty to move around in this enormous wild country.

"Hi-yi! G'long! Hi-yi!" Danny shouted at his mules.

"Hi-yi! Hi-yi! Hi-yi!" screamed Caleb who was riding perched on the lead mule's collar.

The startled animal gave a jerk forward.

A dismal thought occurred to Danny as he joggled along, waiting for the stage to arrive. Maybe the colonel couldn't —or wouldn't—drive the mules after all. The fact was that Danny didn't know the colonel at all well, certainly not well enough to tell whether he could rely on his word. Come to think of it, he didn't even know for a fact that the colonel could drive two mules, to say nothing of eight.

He had seen Colonel Cluggage for the first time only two days before the wagon train left. Danny had been alone in the print shop when the colonel walked in. One thing he had to say about the colonel. He hadn't wasted any time coming to the point.

"I understand you know how to set type, run a press, and handle mules," he had said. "I've got a good job for you if you'd like to make a career for yourself out West." Then he went on to explain that he had a wagon loaded with printing press, type, and paper which he was taking to Santa Fe where he intended to start a small English-language printing shop. He wasn't a printer himself. He was a businessman. Last year he had toured the West looking for good opportunities, and the printing shop idea was one of several ventures he had decided on. The trouble was that he had lost the man he had hired to drive his wagon and do the printing when they got to Santa Fe. The fellow got drunk and fell off the seat and a wheel went over his leg, breaking it so that he couldn't travel.

Danny hadn't taken much time to check over the press or the wagon—or the colonel, for that matter. He just grabbed the chance that was offered and hoped for the best. So far everything had worked out all right. The wagon was sound, and so were the mules. Danny could only hope that the colonel was a man of his word and would do his share of the driving—and that he was on this coach.

"Ah-whooh-wah!"

The coach pulled rapidly closer. Now Danny saw the driver wearing the customary air of disdain that stage drivers had for the lowly mule skinners. As the coach rattled and lurched by, Danny peered anxiously at the faces in the open windows, but he couldn't tell whether the colonel's was one of them. The horses dashed on toward the very head of the train where Major Adams rode a little to one side. Suddenly the driver pulled the coach to a stop. The door opened and a man stepped out. Then the horses were off again before a carpetbag, tossed from the top of the coach, had touched the ground.

"Caleb!" Danny cried. "It's him. It must be! Who else would be leaving the coach out here in the middle of nowhere? Hi-yi! G'long!"

By the time the stagecoach disappeared over the top of a rise, Danny caught up with Major Adams and a tall, slender man wearing a stovepipe hat, cutaway coat, and dark trousers.

"Colonel!" Danny shouted.

The man turned, and Danny was startled by what he saw. This wasn't the clean-shaven, neat gentleman who had hired him in Independence. A ten-day growth of black beard appeared above a shirt that might have been white once but now was covered with prairie dust that sweat had turned to mud. The black hat and suit looked equally disreputable. And the eyes that stared at Danny were hollow, bloodshot, and weary.

Amused by the look on Danny's face, the man said cheerily, "I'm certainly glad to see you—and to get out of that coach. Riding in it day and night for ten days is more than flesh can bear."

Major Adams smiled. "You joined us at the right time if you want to go slow for a while. We aren't exactly going to gallop up over Raton Pass."

"Any place where I can wash off a few layers of dirt?" the colonel asked.

"If you want to clean yourself up fancy, you can do it in a saloon in Trinidad," the major answered. "We'll stop on the other side of the town about noon. But if you want to do the way we do, you can wash yourself and your clothes at the same time. We'll be crossing Raton Creek fifty-three times before we get to the top of the pass."

"Thanks, Major." Colonel Cluggage handed his carpetbag to Danny who pushed it through the opening in the canvas wagon top.

As the colonel climbed aboard, Danny tried to think just how he ought to bring up the subject of driving from here on. But Major Adams must have known what was on Danny's mind, for he solved the problem on the spot.

"Colonel," the major said, "I'll be getting along now. One thing before I move on: You made a good choice when you hired Danny Green. He's brought your wagon through in good shape. And it hasn't been easy. I expect he'd appreciate it if you took the reins for a while and let him ride one of those frisky horses of yours. He's been wanting to keep my scout company. And it wouldn't be a bad idea to double up on the scouting for the next few days. There's talk that the Utes may be up to something."

"Certainly, Major. Danny, I thank you for your loyalty." The colonel smiled as he talked in his soft southern drawl.

"I checked up on you in Independence, and they told me to expect the best. I'll be glad to drive right after our noonday stop."

Danny had a sudden picture of his employer sitting in the driver's seat—stovepipe hat, cutaway coat, and all— trying to get some action out of these ornery mules. He almost laughed, and then he had an awful thought. Maybe the colonel didn't know a thing about mules. How could this city man handle an eight-mule team?

But it turned out Danny didn't have to worry. Colonel Cluggage had obviously done a good bit of mule skinning in his day. When he came back from his noonday visit to the village of Trinidad he was not only clean and shaven, but he had exchanged his city clothes for red flannel shirt, blue jean pants, and broad-brimmed felt hat of the sort that wagoners wore. Except for his beardless face and his soft white hands, you couldn't have told him from the professional mule skinners in the train.

"All right, Danny, my boy," he said cheerfully. "Fetch old Tennessee from the cavvyard. My saddle is in the wagon, isn't it?"

"Yes, sir," Danny answered. He pulled the drawstring that held the canvas top closed at the rear.

"I'll just see how the stuff is riding," the colonel said, and he climbed up to look in. The next moment he exclaimed, "Shoo! Get out of here!"

"Hi, Danny!" a croaking voice replied.

Danny burst out laughing and barely managed to gasp, "Colonel, I forgot to introduce you. That's Caleb, my crow."

Colonel Cluggage retreated from the wagon, holding a beautiful Mexican saddle.

"Where was that bird all morning?" the colonel asked curiously.

"Oh, around. He visits other wagons. Everybody feeds him."

"Well, that's a new one—a crow in a wagon train," the colonel remarked in a light tone of voice. He seemed determined to fit himself into whatever patterns of behavior had been established. Danny was glad. Some men who had been tired by a long stagecoach ride would have got cranky about the least little thing that was out of the ordinary.

"Come on, Caleb. We're going places!" Danny tapped his shoulder, the signal for the crow to perch there.

Caleb left his roost in the space between the top of the cargo and the canvas cover and glided down onto Danny's shoulder.

"That's pretty good!" Colonel Cluggage exclaimed. "A crow as smart as that—I'll bet you could teach him to set type!"

"Oh, he knows a lot about helping around a print shop already," Danny answered, grinning. But a cautious streak in him warned that it might not be wise to let the colonel know that Caleb loved to steal type and hide it away in odd spots.

Danny went off with the saddle, and before long he was astride Tennessee, the tall gray gelding, ready to join Flint at the head of the wagon train, blessedly free of worries about the unpredictable behavior of mules.

"What are we waiting for?" he asked when he realized that neither Flint nor the wagon train was getting started for the afternoon run.

"Orders," Flint replied cryptically, and Danny had the

galling experience of having to kill time as he stood on the threshold of the freedom he had been looking forward to.

It wasn't long, actually, before the major appeared and explained a little, at least, about the delay.

"A young Army captain got hold of me in Trinidad. He was feeling mighty important. Ordered me, mind you *ordered* me, not to move until he got all the big words out of his system and he was down to the ordinary two-for-a-nickel variety even you and I can understand."

"What did he want?" Flint asked.

"Seems the Army is worried about these Utes. They're gathering on the other side of the pass in Eagle Park."

"What for?" Danny asked. "Are they on the warpath?"

"Oh, I doubt it," the major answered, with such elaborate calmness Danny felt sure he wasn't telling the truth.

"Wasn't it near Trinidad that the Utes tore things up about this time last year?" Flint asked.

"That's why the captain is there, I guess," the major said. "We'll be smart to keep our eyes open. The fact is, until this scare dies down, the Army is making all wagon trains from the East take the Cimarron Crossing. We're the last they're going to let through over the mountain route for a while."

"Hmm," said Flint.

The major looked sharply at Danny and then at Danny's rifle that lay across his lap. "You aren't trigger-happy, are you, boy?" he asked. "My guess is that we won't have any trouble with the Utes unless we start it. But if any of us get excited and start shooting, there might be a real mess."

This, Danny thought, could mean only one thing. There *were* Indians ahead and the major *was* worried.

"I sure enough don't want to start anything," Danny said, and he meant it. "I'll stick close to Flint and do what he says."

Flint grinned at him. "Let's go, kid. It's a fine day for a ride."

At first Danny rode in silence at Flint's side, enjoying the clear mountain stream they were following. For the first time in six weeks trees surrounded him, and it was cool in the shade. And for the first time since they had left Independence, he thought, the trail began to look as if some work had been done on it. Big rocks had been pulled to one side; ledges had been blasted off. In one place there was even a log bridge.

Flint broke the silence. "Indians have been along here."

"How do you know?" Danny asked.

Flint pointed at the ground. "See those hoofprints? Indian ponies made them."

Danny thought they looked like any old hoofprints, and his face must have showed the fact.

"Sure, look at them," Flint went on. "Our horses and mules are shod. But Indian ponies aren't—unless they have recently been stolen. These fellows can't be far ahead of us. They went along here after the stagecoach. You can see the hoofprints on top of the wheel tracks."

Danny wasn't interested in details. He felt aquiver with excitement that Indians were near. What would he do— what should he do—if he met them? Before he found an answer, Caleb zoomed out of the sky and struck his shoulder with claws that clutched painfully through his shirt. The crow seemed alarmed and scolded in Danny's ear. Several times he flapped up into the air a little way, then settled back down.

"What's wrong with *him?*" Flint asked.

"You tell me," Danny answered in a low voice. "He's seen something that scared him. Do you suppose it's Indians?"

"Why should they scare a crow, even if he did see them?" Flint raised his eyes and scanned the sky. "Say, that's what frightened him, probably. Look!"

Half a dozen huge ravens slowly circled and swooped close to the treetops on the ridge above the trail.

"Caleb, you disgraceful coward!" Danny said, laughing. "Just because they're bigger than you are—"

Flint interrupted: "We may have stumbled onto something, Danny. I have a hunch those ravens mean there's an Indian camp over the hill. You almost always see them near a camp waiting to clean up the bones and leavings."

Ravens weren't the only scavengers around. Danny caught a glimpse of a gray coyote slinking through the trees on the ridge.

"Well, what do we do?"

"Ride over real friendly and get acquainted. One thing, don't make any sudden moves. Somebody just might be suspicious and take a shot at us."

Flint searched the hillside for signs of a trail, but finding none, urged Chiquita, his fast little sorrel horse, up the steep, open slope. Danny, ten yards or so behind, saw Flint come out onto the ridge, and then Chiquita suddenly shied. Danny reined in, waiting for a signal, while the ravens circled and screamed overhead.

"All right, come on," Flint said quietly. "Bad business here."

Soon enough Danny saw what he meant. And it was not the Indian camp Flint had expected to find. The ravens had been circling over something much more alarming. On the ground just ahead lay a horse. Beside it lay a man—an Indian. Both were dead.

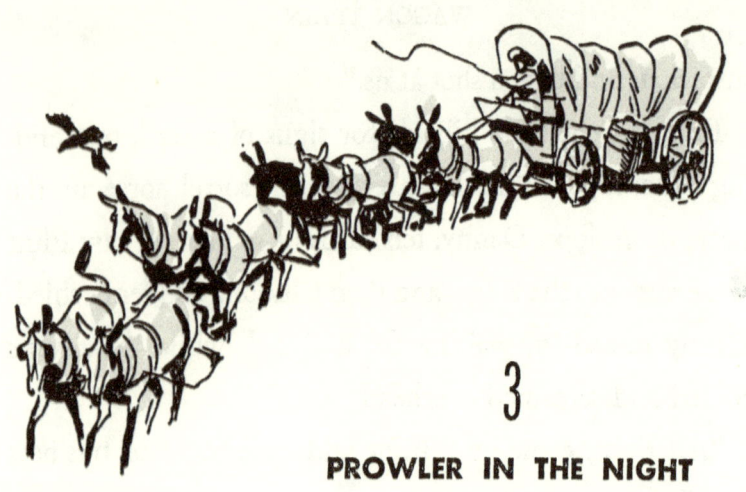

3

PROWLER IN THE NIGHT

Danny's heart felt like a startled wild thing inside him. It shied and leaped and quivered—just as his horse was doing.

A dead Indian, where he had expected to find a village of live ones! A dead Indian, and not only that. Ravens and coyotes had begun to tear at the flesh. Danny couldn't take his eyes from the grisly spectacle.

"What happened?" He intended to whisper the words, but they burst out of him with a croaking sound.

"This is bad medicine," Flint muttered, almost to himself. And when Danny glanced up, he could see that the scout was shaken.

"Who killed him, do you think? Why—" Danny asked.

Flint didn't answer at once. Instead he swung to the ground. Holding his nervous horse tightly, he approached the body.

And now little details that Danny would never forget fixed themselves in his mind: the dead Indian's skin, so dark it was almost black—the broad face—the two thick braids of jet black hair, each wrapped in the middle with white buckskin—the elk-tooth necklace—the buckskin trousers half covered by a long-tailed, red flannel shirt.

"The Utes are going to think some white man did it," Flint said, still as if he were thinking out loud.

"Well, who did?"

"Nobody. Nobody killed him," Flint answered.

Did Flint mean that the man had shot himself?

"Nobody killed him, but we have to convince the Utes of it, so they won't attack us in revenge." Flint looked up. "Here, hold Chiquita, Danny."

He handed Danny the reins and strode past the Indian's dead horse toward an object that lay on the ground several yards away. Danny had all he could do to control Chiquita and Tennessee. The odor of death—or the sight in front of them—or something had sent panic through the two animals.

Flint was back in a moment holding the strangest-looking rifle Danny had even seen. The barrel and the stock were encased in horsehide with red and white pinto markings on it. Dangling from the muzzle hung strips of leather and eagle feathers. But the breech of the rifle was only a mass of torn metal.

The peculiar gun threw Chiquita into new panic. Not until Flint had calmed her and swung into the saddle could he begin to explain what he thought the extraordinary scene meant.

"That Ute and his horse were killed by lightning," he said. "Yesterday. Maybe in the same storm that hit us. He was up on a high place where lightning is likely to strike, and it did. The bolt exploded the cartridges in the breech of his rifle. Blew it all to pieces."

"Well!" Danny exclaimed in relief. "They can't say white men killed him."

"That's where you're wrong, Danny. In another couple

of hours the ravens and coyotes will see to it that nothing is left up here on the ridge but some bones and an elk-tooth necklace that a certain Ute was known to wear. The bones will be close to the trail. The Utes are bound to find them and think that the Indian and his mount were targets for some trigger-happy wagoner. And that could mean plenty of trouble for us, or for some other party of emigrants."

Danny shivered a little.

"Now here's what we're going to do: We'll push on up the trail as fast as we can to Uncle Dick Wootton's place. We'll tell our story to him and ask him to pass it along to the Utes the best way he can. We'll leave him the gun. The Indians will recognize it. I never saw one wrapped this way myself. The exploded breech may help to convince them that lightning really killed the man."

"Good!" Danny sighed. Flint's explanation of the tragedy and his clear plan to avert trouble gave him a feeling of great relief.

"After we see Wootton, we'll go back and tell the major."

"Shouldn't we bury the Indian?" Danny asked.

"I think so, but Uncle Dick and the major will have to

decide that. Different tribes have different customs about burial. It might go against the Utes' beliefs for us to do it."

"Hi, Danny!" came a rasping voice from overhead. "Holy Moses!"

"Caleb, you scoundrel!" Danny had been so occupied with discovering the dead Indian and handling the spooky horses that he had forgotten his crow.

Flint watched Caleb sail down onto Danny's shoulder. "That bird may be smart, but he won't win any medals for bravery. He's been hiding in a tree where the ravens couldn't see him."

Danny looked up. Sure enough, the great black birds still circled overhead, waiting for the intruders to leave.

Alternating between a trot and a fast walk, Flint rode Chiquita hard up the wagon road which switched back and forth and rose rapidly between canyon walls. Danny followed in silence while Caleb perched on the saddle horn with occasional cautious flights overhead. At last they emerged onto a kind of wide bench in the mountainside.

"We're over the worst of it," Flint said. "Let's take a breather."

"Flint, what was that Indian doing on the ridge back there? He had a good view of the road. Maybe he was scouting for a war party when the thunderstorm came."

"He might have been watching the road, all right. But I doubt if he was a member of a war party. He didn't wear any paint or the decorations that most of these Indians do when they're up to something big. He was dressed just average, and he had a shirt on. I've heard that Utes on the warpath usually strip to the waist."

"I hope you're right." Danny couldn't imagine a worse place to be attacked than in the canyon they had just left.

Within an hour they came out into a pleasant little mountain park. Ahead Danny saw a barn and a massive house which reminded him vaguely of pictures he had seen of mansions on southern plantations. The road at one point beyond was effectively blocked with a chain.

"Here we are," Flint said. "This is where Uncle Dick collects his tolls."

Danny knew the story of Uncle Dick Wootton. The famous old frontiersman had carved this road up over Raton Pass and then started charging everybody a toll to use it—everybody except the Indians. This didn't reflect any special love of Indians. It was simply that Uncle Dick despaired of explaining to them why they should pay *him* to cross land that had always belonged to *them* and, so far as they were concerned, still did.

Before long Danny and Flint had their horses tied to the hitching bar near the house.

"Uncle Dick here?" Flint asked a nondescript old fellow lounging against a porch post.

"Yep." The man nodded, jerking a thumb at the door.

"Somebody looking for me?" a voice boomed. "Come on in!"

The sole occupant of the big room was a burly man who had a great shock of black hair tinged with gray. The room itself was a jumble of rough plank tables, benches, and packing boxes. Nailed to the walls were deer antlers, big-horn sheep heads, buffalo skulls, and skins. Bearskins, including one that must have come from a grizzly, were flung about over the boxes and barrels.

"What can I do for you young fellows?" the big man boomed at them.

Flint introduced himself and quickly told how he and Danny had discovered the dead Ute. Uncle Dick Wootton whistled when Flint produced the curiously decorated rifle. "That was once a good weapon. Somebody must've swiped it from the Army. Most of the Utes don't have guns, you know. They still use bows and arrows."

Danny felt a small shiver of excitement. Somehow an arrow seemed much more frightening than a bullet. And somewhere in the hills nearby were men who might take a notion to use their arrows.

After a minute's thought Uncle Dick said, "I'll ride on toward the pass and catch the Utes who were here today. I'll tell 'em your story. Meantime, you go on back. I guess it would be a good idea if Major Adams had the warrior buried. The Utes don't care much for handling the dead. They bury their people at night and in secret when they can. They'll be glad enough if you take care of it for 'em, I expect."

"Good," said Flint.

"The way I'll tell the story," Uncle Dick went on, "it will sound like you're trying to be friendly." The big man paused and then launched into a different line of thought. "You say you're with Seth Adams' wagon train? How's that old porcupine been acting since yesterday? Kind of prickly?"

Danny saw a look of caution cross Flint's face, as the scout said, "Did you by any chance talk to the captain of that wagon train that came through here a little while ago?"

Uncle Dick exploded with loud guffaws. "Never thought I'd see *anybody* pass old Seth on the trail! Time was when he wouldn't let a stampeding herd of buffalo get by him, unless of course it was Sunday, which is his day for being polite. Tell me, is that old sinner still as full of pious sayings and secondhand advice as he used to be?" After another hearty laugh, Uncle Dick strode toward his barn to get a horse for the errand he had promised to run.

"Holy Moses!" Caleb squawked as he dropped down out of a tree and landed on Danny's shoulder.

"Holy Moses is right," Danny replied, chuckling. This had been quite a day, and every once in a while on the ride back down the canyon he shook his head and muttered, "Holy Moses!"

When at last they rejoined the train, the wagons were all circled up for the night.

"I was worried about you, son," Major Adams said to Flint. Then he listened quietly to the scout's report. "Well, you did right to go on up to Wootton's place," he said after Flint ended his story. "Never put off till tomorrow what you can do today. I'll send a couple of men to take care of the Ute burial. And just to be on the safe side, we'll double the guard again tonight."

This meant that Danny's turn at guard duty would come right after he had had something to eat. He had assumed that Colonel Cluggage would be at the campfire, anxiously awaiting his return, or at least the return of Tennessee and the valuable saddle. But the colonel, like the other men who ate at the major's campfire, had finished his meal and gone off. In fact, Danny discovered, the colonel was already sound asleep under the wagon—which wasn't surprising in view of his long stagecoach ride and a half-day's mule skinning to top it off.

Danny filled his plate with the inevitable beans, bacon, and biscuits. A moment later Flint turned up to get his supper, and at his heels came a tousle-haired barefoot boy and a pig-tailed girl, also barefoot.

"Here we go again," Danny called with a grin. "Beans, bacon, biscuits, Bizz and Buzz."

Every night at this time the youngsters, who were twins and the only children in the wagon train, appeared at the major's campfire, insisting that Flint tell them the story of his day's adventures. And almost always they began with the same question: "Did you see any Indians?"

But tonight Flint said first, "I've got a surprise for you. I *did* see an Indian. So did Danny. He went with me. Tell 'em about it, Danny."

The little girl planted herself in front of Danny, arms akimbo, swishing her long gray skirt. "Tell us about it."

"All right, Bizz. But let me get something in my stomach first." Danny ate slowly, while he decided what to say. He didn't want to scare the kids; they were only nine-year-olds, after all. Plainly Flint didn't want to either. That was why the scout had ducked out and asked Danny to report on the Indian. Of course, Danny did know the kids better than Flint did. They often came to ride in his wagon, and they never got tired of talking to Caleb.

Bizz waited for what doubtless seemed to her a long time, while Danny took two bites. "What kind of Indian did you see?" she asked.

"Ute," he muttered with his mouth full. Then, deciding to get it over with, he went on to describe the Indian and the horse in great detail, carefully omitting the fact that they had been dead. As he talked, Danny surprised himself. He hadn't realized how much he had noticed about the horse in the few tension-filled minutes he had spent on the ridge. "It was a white horse," he said. "The Indian rode it bareback. And you know what? He rode with only one rein and no bit."

"You can't ride that way," Bizz said.

"Indians can. They just tie a rope or a strip of rawhide around the lower jaw. There's a space between a horse's teeth where a rope can fit. All right, that's all there is about the Indian." Danny stood up. "I have to go and do guard duty now."

"You left out something," Buzz, the little boy, said in a flat, matter-of-fact voice. "You should have said the Indian

was dead. That's what Major Adams told Daddy. Daddy went to dig him a grave."

Danny shrugged. He should have known better. It was no use trying to fool the children. Even Buzz, who always trailed a little behind Bizz, kept up with just about everything that went on.

Major Adams stationed the guards at strategic points around the camp, which had been drawn up in a little glade at the bottom of the V-shaped canyon. It fell to Danny's lot to be a sentry on one of the ridges that rose on either side. With his gun sometimes on his shoulder, more often in his hand at his side, he paced back and forth under the big pine trees and peered constantly in all the directions from which Indians might approach. It was no use listening for them. The wind made such a moaning and whirring in the trees that all but the sharpest sounds were covered up. Except for an occasional bray from a mule, only one distinguishable noise came from the camp. That was the voice of Mrs. Gower, the children's mother, calling, "Beatrice! Barnabus! Bedtime!" This was followed by, "In a minute!" from Bizz and Buzz. Danny could bet the

twins' mother would have trouble getting them to bed tonight. For the first time in the whole trip they had camped
beside a clearwater stream. Cold though it was, Raton
Creek was twice as much fun to paddle in as the muddy
Arkansas.

Danny glanced down at the circle of wagons. The camp-
fires glowed cheerfully in the dusk that began to fill the
canyon. In the corral formed by the wagons some of the
horses and mules grazed hungrily. The rest of the stock,
hobbled so that they couldn't get far away, were pastured
for the night a little way upstream, and a couple of guards
were on duty to watch them. The whole scene looked so
peaceful that Danny was almost lulled into forgetting why
he was up here on the ridge watching it. Sternly he reminded himself that *he* had found an *Indian* lookout today, just
a little farther along this same ridge.

Dusk turned to darkness, and Danny now walked with
his gun held lightly in both hands in front of him. This
position would save a split second if he needed to raise the
rifle and fire. If only he could see better, if only the wind
in the trees would stop so he could hear. . . .

Danny focused all the intense energy he had in an effort to pick out definable objects in the gloom under the trees, trying to separate one sound from another in the general murmur of the night. Was that a footstep? He was sure he felt a thump on the earth along the hillside. No. He was trying so hard that he had dreamed up the sensation. In spite of himself he felt rather than heard another vibration in the earth beneath his feet, as if a step had been taken. "Get hold of yourself!" he thought, peering all around. No unfamiliar shape was to be seen.

Snap! From immediately behind came the dry, sharp report of a breaking branch. Danny whirled around. "Who's there?" he called out.

Instead of an answer there was only a dark figure that lunged toward him. The next instant Danny fired—and fired again. The figure slumped and fell.

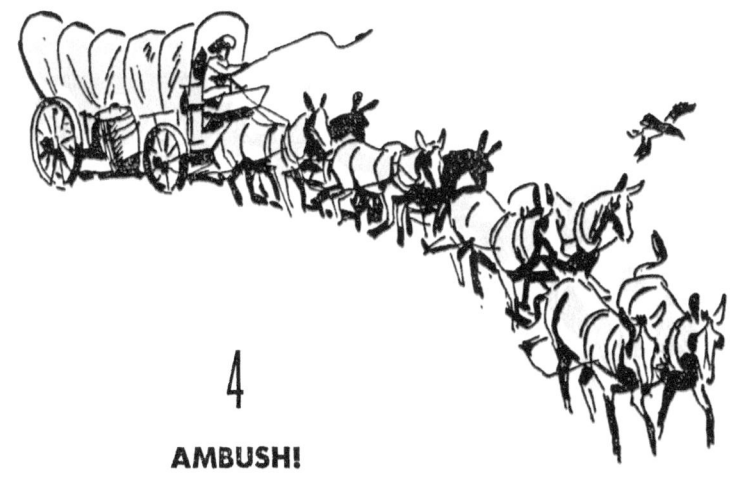

4

AMBUSH!

Terrified though he was, Danny approached the prowler
he had shot. In the dim starlight he studied the outlines of
the body on the ground. It was not a Ute. He had shot a
horse or a mule! By the time Major Adams and Flint
reached the top of the ridge, he was wishing he had some
magic formula that would make him disappear into the
night.

The major simply poked the dead mule with his foot
and said, "I never knew it to fail. There's always some
trigger-happy galoot that tries to save the world from the
Indians by shooting up the stock."

Danny was too ashamed even to say he was sorry. He

stood there, a solid lump of misery and embarrassment, until the major gave him a whack on the shoulder and said, "Did it myself once. Now go on down and get some sleep. Flint'll stay and take your place."

Choking with a mixture of remorse and relief, Danny stumbled down the hill and found his way to his buffalo robe which he had already spread out on the ground under the wagon. In a moment he was as sound asleep as the weary Colonel Cluggage, who apparently hadn't been awakened by the hubbub Danny's shot had caused in the camp.

Danny woke with a groan. He knew what he would have to face. The whole wagon train was going to tease him about the "Indian" he had shot last night. And he was right. Off and on all day he had to put up with jokes. The colonel had decided he didn't care to drive the mules two days running. So Danny couldn't even get away from it all by riding out ahead with Flint. He did, however, get the colonel to agree that he could go with Flint every second day.

The climb up the pass was a slow, tough struggle for the

mules. Danny had all he could do to manage them, and there was no time to wonder whether Indians were watching the progress of the wagon train.

The only break came during the noon stop at Uncle Dick Wootton's place, and that was a disappointment because Uncle Dick wasn't there. Flint and Danny couldn't find out what had happened when he delivered the dead Ute's gun to the horsemen he had set out yesterday to overtake. Worst of all, Danny was horrified to find that his fame had spread even to the toll taker who removed the chain from across the toll road.

"I hear you shot yourself a mule last night," the old fellow said.

Danny winced and nodded.

"It happens to the best of us," the man went on cheerfully. "I guess you know the major killed his own favorite horse once. Now me, I never shot a horse or a mule in my life. But I did shoot me a mighty scraggly blind old bull buffalo one night, thinking it was a Comanche." He cackled and ran his fingers through the white hair that hung down to his shoulders.

Danny handed over the three fifty-cent pieces that Colonel Cluggage had given him to pay the toll. The old man dropped them onto the heap of coins in his broad-brimmed hat on the ground at his feet and yelled to the mules, "Hi-yi! G' long!"

Danny cracked his whip, and on they went, still climbing. To his surprise the pass itself was not the rugged affair he had imagined a mountain pass would be. There was a broad meadow, well watered and deep in grass in spite of all the animals that had stopped there to graze this summer.

"Fort up!" the major ordered, and the wagons slowly rumbled into place. With the front wheels of one wagon overlapping the back wheels of the next in line, they made their usual circle for protection against attack.

Danny had hobbled the mules and turned them loose when he felt a tug at his sleeve. It was Bizz with a frightened look on her face. In her wake as usual stood Buzz, solemn and scared.

"Danny! Come!" Bizz whispered. "Bring your gun. Indians."

Dog take it! thought Danny. Things were going too far

when even the twins tried to rib him about last night. But a second look at Bizz convinced him that joking was the last thing in the world she had in mind. Her face, underneath the dirt and sunburn, was actually a pale green! She had seen something that scared her right down the middle!

Still, just to make sure, Danny decided to see for himself before he raised any alarm. He followed her, and fifty yards from the wagons she motioned him to lie down and look over the top of a little knoll.

There, in a part of the meadow not visible from the wagon train, were four mounted Indians, apparently having a discussion while their horses nibbled at the grass.

"Go get the major!" Danny whispered. "And Flint! Hurry now!"

The twins scampered off, and Danny raised his head for a long, careful look. He could scarcely believe what he saw. The biggest of the four horsemen was wearing what could only be a stovepipe hat, the kind that Colonel Cluggage had worn when he arrived on the stagecoach. Aside from this one bizarre bit of costume, however, the Indians had on the drabbest kind of old clothes. Nor were they painted up. If what Flint said yesterday was true, these men weren't on the warpath.

Before long the twins came scurrying back and flopped down, one on each side of Danny.

"You watch what's going to happen!" Bizz said. Fear had left her face but excitement hadn't yet brought back all the color to it.

Danny did watch. Almost immediately Major Adams and Flint appeared on their horses, riding with right hands high above their heads, palm forward. The Indians replied with a similar gesture. The major handed each of the Indians a large chunk of red cloth, and then all six men began a most astonishing performance.

"What are they doing?" Bizz asked.

"Talking in sign language," Danny replied. He glanced at Buzz and chuckled. The little boy had got to his knees and was practicing the gestures he saw across the meadow. "What are you up to, Buzz?" Danny asked.

"Flint's got to teach me that," was the answer.

"So you and Bizz can talk without being told to keep still, is that it?"

The brilliance of this notion dawned on Bizz who exploded into sound: "Yippee-yippee-yippee-yippee!" It was her special way of showing enthusiasm.

Danny tagged along with Buzz when Bizz picked up her skirts and ran to meet the major and Flint. He wanted to hear the answers to the questions he knew the little girl was going to ask.

For once the major had an answer ready before she got anything asked. "Know who I was talking to?" he said. "Two Ute chiefs. And they're twins, by golly! The big fat fellow with the stovepipe hat is named Kanneatche and the skinny little fellow is his twin brother Curicata."

"Major! You're joking," Bizz protested.

"Young lady, I am telling the gospel truth," the major said. "They are twins—two of the biggest Ute chiefs. They told me, what's more, that they aren't on the warpath. You know what I answered?"

Buzz spoke up. "You said you aren't on the warpath either."

The major looked a little startled. "As a matter of fact, I did say something like that. I told them we're just passing through their country, and we don't intend to stay or cause them any trouble."

"But why is he wearing that fancy hat? That's for white men," Bizz said. "Indians are supposed to wear feathers."

"Why does your mother wear feathers in her Sunday hat? Is she an Indian?" the major asked.

This made Bizz turn thoughtful. It was a while before she had anything to say.

"Flint," Buzz demanded, "teach me sign language."

"All right. Sometime when I'm not too busy. Tomorrow, if I have time."

After supper, when Colonel Cluggage had gone off to take his turn at guard duty, Bizz and Buzz appeared, bringing Caleb some leftover beans. The twins climbed to the seat of the *Poor Richard,* and while the crow ate, they began to pretend they were talking sign language. Presently Bizz laughed. Danny looked up.

Bizz held out her hand and dropped three fifty-cent pieces down to Danny. "I told Buzz you've been sitting on these to hatch 'em. You're trying to hatch 'em out into a mess of two-bit pieces."

"Where did you get those?" Danny asked.

"Right here on the seat. Didn't you know?"

"They must have dropped out of the colonel's pocket," Danny said. "I'll give them back to him."

"Those don't belong to the colonel," Buzz said slowly. "They belong to Caleb. He put them there. I saw him."

"Where did the scoundrel get them?" Danny asked.

"He took them out of the man's hat—the man who had a hat full of money back there at the gate."

Danny shook his fist at Caleb who had been perched on the canvas wagon top watching the activities of the twins. "You son of a thundergust!" he shouted. "Somebody's going to make you into a stew, if you keep on stealing things. How am I going to get that money back to the man?"

"Abe Lincoln walked," Buzz said.

"Oh, rats!" Danny exclaimed. What a literal-minded little cuss Buzz was!

"Give it to the major. He'll know what to do," Bizz suggested.

Danny did just that. The major laughed and said he would see that the money was returned to the tollgate keeper. There was no question of Danny's walking or even riding back down to Wootton's tonight. Not a soul was to leave camp. Much as the major liked the twin Ute chiefs, he suspected that some of the warriors in their band might not be above a little highway robbery. But more serious was the likelihood that a road agent pretending to be a Ute might waylay a lone rider. People had been murdered in this country for a lot less than a horse and a gun and a dollar-fifty. So Danny dozed off, happy that he didn't have to be as honest as Abe Lincoln, that night at least. As sleep was coming, the strange wail of coyotes filled the night. The real sound of their wailing blended into a dream—a dream in which the coyote calls were being made by Indians who lurked near the mountain meadow, signaling to each other as they prepared to attack.

Danny recalled it again and again the next day while he and Flint helped each of the drivers in turn to get their wagons down the steepest and most difficult sections of the road. But in spite of all precautions, two wagons tipped over. Their freight spilled out, and Major Adams fumed at the delay. The major had a reputation for bringing his

trains through on a good, fast, safe schedule, and he wanted
to keep it. Danny knew that it wasn't only the possibility
of trouble with the Utes that caused the big, gruff man's
irritation. The major was still riled because the rival wagon
train had passed him and might now beat him in to Santa
Fe.

The time they lost that day was more than made up the
following day. The major refused to let anyone stop even
for a few minutes at the log cabin and barn which was a
station where the stagecoach changed horses, although he
did send Flint over to pick up whatever news he could.

The Utes, Flint reported, were continuing to gather.
Their camp was believed to be in Eagle Park, to the south
and west. Several wagon trains had reported the loss of
stock. Nobody seemed to know whether the horse thieves
were Indians or the gang of rustlers that operated in the
area. As for other news, they still hadn't caught the bandit
who had pulled off the big jewel robbery in Santa Fe.

"Flint," Danny said, "did you find out anything about
the other train? Are we gaining on it?"

"To tell you the truth, I forgot about it and I didn't ask

at the coach stop," Flint replied.

"Well, do you think we're gaining?"

"I wouldn't be surprised."

As they rode along ahead of the train, Danny kept hoping he would hear the rumbling wheels of their rival's train. Instead, he heard the unmistakable sound of half a dozen rifle shots.

"What's that mean?" he asked.

"It might be something—it might be nothing," was Flint's reply. But Danny noticed that the scout checked his rifle, just in case it proved to be "something."

Presently they came around the end of a low hill, and Danny saw a green patch—sure sign of water. A little mountain stream apparently came out of a canyon to their right.

"This place looks made to order for an ambush," Danny said.

"Um-hum," Flint answered. Then, as if he had been struck a sharp blow, "Stop, Danny! Look!"

Not far from the stream stood a covered wagon that had been coming their way. Four mules had been pulling it.

But they lay sprawled out in strangely twisted positions, still in harness. And sticking from the faded blue side of the wagon bed Danny could see the feathered shafts of Indian arrows!

5

A PUZZLING RESCUE

"Keep your eyes peeled!" Flint said in a low voice. Moving cautiously, he led the way toward the blue wagon.

Danny dug his heels into Tennessee's quivering sides, as the horse held back and tried to sidle away.

"Those shots we heard," Danny whispered, "they killed the mules."

Flint nodded.

"I wonder what happened to the driver?"

Flint shook his head.

Danny found himself wishing somehow he could find a place with a wall behind him, so that he only had to look out in one direction. He had a feeling he would be shot at from behind, no matter which way he faced.

"Anybody here?" Flint called without warning, and Danny jumped. "Hey! Anybody in the wagon?"

There was no answer.

"I'd better take a look anyway," Flint told Danny.

But before he had time to dismount, a forehead rose cautiously in the front opening of the white wagon top. A bearded face appeared, followed by a heavy-set body. The man looked like the eastern farmers Danny used to see going through Independence on their way west.

"You all right?" Flint called.

The man nodded, obviously speechless with fear.

"Anybody else here? Anybody hurt?"

"No," the man croaked. "I'm alone."

"How many were in the war party? Which way did they go?"

"Must have been fifteen or twenty of 'em. Only about six had rifles. The rest had bows and arrows. They took off thataway." He pointed a shaky finger upstream. "One of 'em was just getting into the wagon—to scalp me, I guess—but then I heard some sort of a hullabaloo. Maybe there was a lookout that saw you fellows coming. Anyway, they lit out in a hurry. I guess I'm just plain lucky." There was silence for a moment. "That's funny, though. Why do you suppose just the two of you would scare all of them off?"

"We're scouting for Major Adams' wagon train," Flint answered. "If their lookout was up on the hill there, maybe he could see the train as well as us."

"I guess that's it." The man drew a deep breath and climbed down from his wagon, plainly feeling better. "My name's Tunis Teel. I'd like to shake your hands, young fellows."

Danny felt a sudden rush of pity for this lone emigrant who seemed so confused and helpless and grateful for his rescue from the Indians, although Flint and Danny hadn't really done a thing to help him.

"Danny," Flint said thoughtfully, "I don't like this, but it has to be the way I say. I've got standing orders in a case like this. I have to go back and notify the major at once. I want you to stay here with Mr. Teel. Both of you get into the wagon, one at each end, and keep a sharp lookout.

I don't think anything will happen. But if the Indians do come back, you can hold them off long enough for me and the major to get here with some of the men."

"Sure, Flint. You go on," Danny gulped. He was suddenly very frightened. It seemed certain that Mr. Teel needed him, but he wasn't at all sure he would get any help at all out of Mr. Teel in a pinch.

Nervously Danny climbed up and into the wagon bed. To his surprise the wagon was almost empty. And when Mr. Teel picked up his rifle and squatted down on what seemed to be a bedroll in the rear, Danny couldn't help blurting out the question that puzzled him: "How come you're out here all by yourself, Mr. Teel? Most folks don't care to travel through this country alone."

"Well, son, I'll tell you." The man was relaxing and shaking off his terror. But his story came out in disjointed phrases, parts of it in queer order, and what Danny managed to unscramble went something like this: Mr. Teel had left his farm in Pennsylvania to come west and seek his fortune. About two days' travel distance farther along the trail he had decided he'd had enough of the West. He

didn't like it, and he was going back to Pennsylvania. So he had ignored all advice, sold off most of his equipment, turned around, and started east. He reached this place and was about to make camp when he was attacked by Indians, before he had even had a chance to unhitch his mules.

All the while Danny listened to Mr. Teel's story, he lay propped up on one elbow, looking out through the front opening in the canvas top of the wagon. The thick boards on either side and in front of him gave him some feeling of protection, although he knew very well that a bullet could pierce the wood.

Danny glanced for an instant at Mr. Teel, who kept watch at the rear of the wagon through the opening in the canvas. "I still don't see why you turned around after you'd come such a long way."

"It took me a while to get fed up. But just look at this country!" The Pennsylvanian had disgust in his voice. "The farther you go the drier it gets. I'm a farmer. Land like this is no place for me."

"You're sure in a pickle now," Danny said. "It looks to me as if you'll have to go home on the stagecoach. You can't stay around here, anyway."

There was a silence. Mr. Teel seemed to be puzzling out what he could do. "Has the wagon train got any extra mules or horses in its cavvyard?" he asked finally.

"A few," Danny answered. "Why?"

"Good!" Mr. Teel sounded almost enthusiastic. "That settles it. If I can buy four of 'em, I'll be on my way tomorrow."

On his way? Danny wondered what the man meant. He had said he didn't want to go west, but would he be crazy enough to insist on traveling east alone? "You'll be joining up with our train, then?"

"I'm going home, I told you."

What a stubborn fool! Danny thought. He had heard stories of pioneers facing great danger and hardship in order to settle in the West, but this was the first time he had come up against courage and stubbornness in somebody running *away* from the frontier.

Inwardly Danny made a prophecy that Major Adams would try to get Mr. Teel to accompany his train as far as the next stagecoach station at least.

A sound of hoofbeats made Danny tense up all over. Could it be the Indians returning with reinforcements— or was Flint bringing the major and men from the train? Presently he let out a whoop of relief: It was Flint.

Danny swung down from the wagon. While Mr. Teel told his story to the major, Danny found himself drawn irresistibly to the feathered shafts that stuck out of the side of the wagon. There were four of them, and a tug at one revealed that the stone arrowhead was not very deeply embedded in the wood. Danny pulled it out with a jerk. The others came out easily, but the fourth was deeply wedged in a crack. By the time he managed to work it free, the wagon train had creaked and rattled into sight and had begun to form a circle nearby.

"What's that, Danny? Let me see!" came a shrill voice.

"Let *me* see!" another voice called.

Bizz and Buzz leaped down from their wagon, followed by Caleb who squawked, "Hi, Danny! Holy Moses!"

Smiling, Danny let the twins take his trophies and examine them. The next moment Colonel Cluggage sighted him and summoned him to unhitch the mules.

"You be careful of those arrows," Danny told the twins. "When I get the mules hobbled, I'll tell you where they came from."

Bizz and Buzz couldn't wait. They tagged along behind, spouting questions which Danny managed to answer while at the same time he reported his adventures to Colonel Cluggage.

"Well! I guess this has been quite a day in your life," the colonel said when Danny finished. "You hobble the mules. I'll step over and see if there's anything I can do to help the fellow from Pennsylvania."

The twins, apparently thinking they had squeezed all the excitement possible out of Danny's story, now started toward the stranger who had survived the Indian attack.

"Wait a minute, you little rascals," Danny called. When they returned, he held out his hand. "My arrows."

"Don't be so selfish," Bizz said reproachfully.

"What do you need all of 'em for?" Buzz asked. "You can't shoot 'em."

This was such a reasonable statement that Danny had to laugh. Trust the twins to find a way of getting what they wanted! "All right, you win! Here's one for you, Buzz. And one for you, Bizz. I'm keeping two for myself." Then he added quickly, in order to head off any argument about his division of the spoils, "If you want to know why I need two of them, the answer is I have fifteen reasons. First, I found them. Second, I'm twice as big as you are—"

The twins saw there was no use to protest, and they scampered off toward the crowd that had gathered around the major and Mr. Teel. What they saw and heard there obviously didn't hold their interest very long. Danny saw them examining the arrow holes in Mr. Teel's wagon a minute or two later. By the time he had finished his chores and gone to join the group himself, the youngsters were up inside the wagon, shooting imaginary rifles at imaginary Indians. After a lull in that game, the two of them appeared at Danny's side, their faces pink with excitement.

Bizz snatched Danny's hand and pulled him away from the edge of the crowd around Mr. Teel. "Do you know what? There's a secret hiding place in that wagon!"

"Then why aren't you hiding there?" Danny laughed.

"Silly, it's not big enough! It's just a place under a loose

board in the floor. It's only for hiding *things*."

Feeling a little bit of interest, Danny asked, "What kind of things?"

"All kinds of things. This, for instance!" Bizz triumphantly held out a little buckskin bag.

"Why, you rascal! You put that right back!" Danny exclaimed. "What's in it, anyway?"

"Just a lot of little rocks, it looks like," Bizz answered. She handed Danny the bag.

Feeling guilty, Danny opened the pouch and peered inside as he walked with it toward Mr. Teel's wagon. What he saw looked like tiny pebbles and bits of glass. Quickly then he drew the string and sent Buzz up into the wagon to put the bag back in place. He had heard of wagons that had false bottoms. Years ago smugglers used them to carry illegal stuff from the United States into Santa Fe, which at that time belonged to Mexico. Maybe this was an old smuggler's wagon. It was sure-enough old. Maybe Mr. Teel didn't even know that it had a false bottom! Here was a tempting puzzle to solve. Danny feared his curiosity would get the better of him, as it so often did. He *had* to find a way of discovering what Mr. Teel knew about the peculiar construction of the wagon, and about the little buckskin pouch.

From then on Danny watched the husky Pennsylvania farmer with intense interest. He had plenty of chance because Major Adams invited Mr. Teel to share the evening meal around his campfire.

As usual nobody said a word until the last bean had disappeared along with the last drop of coffee.

The major was the first to speak. "Those mules you bought are pretty thin, Mr. Teel. But they'll take you as far as Fort Union all right. You can rest up there, and maybe you can buy some extra ones before you find a wagon train to join going east."

Well, Danny thought, things had been happening while he was occupied with the pouch the twins had discovered. The major had persuaded the stubborn Teel that his surest way of getting home was to stay alive. And that meant traveling with the major until he got to Fort Union where he would have protection when he dropped out to wait for an eastbound train.

"Yessir," the major said thoughtfully, "those mules are so poor and thin they have to lean up against each other in order to bray. I did have one fat one I could have sold you." He winked at Danny. "But he got into the everlastingest fix."

"How's that?" Mr. Teel asked.

"He got himself shot for an Indian."

Danny winced.

Mr. Teel, of course, couldn't understand what the major meant. "The Indians shot him the way they shot my mules?" he asked.

"No, sir," Danny said quickly. "The major is making fun of me. When I was on guard duty I shot a mule by mistake."

Mr. Teel still seemed a little puzzled, but he turned to Colonel Cluggage and said, "I certainly thank you for letting me have your three extra animals, and I've got no complaints about them. Now what's the name of that backwoods giant who let me have the fourth one?"

Danny knew who fitted that description. It could only be Asa Gower, the father of Bizz and Buzz, six feet three inches tall and skinny as a rail. Everybody in the wagon train said the only difference between Asa Gower and Abe Lincoln was that Asa "hadn't yet got hisself elected President."

"There's something important I didn't have time to talk over with you," Mr. Teel went on earnestly. "I need the mules that you and the other fellow let me have, Colonel. And I'm not objecting to your price. But I guess you can understand how I might not be traveling with *that* much ready cash. I do have something, though, that's just as good as money if you and Mr. Gower are willing to take it."

"Look, my friend," the colonel said, "I don't want to drive a hard bargain with a man who's in trouble. We ought to be able to work out something. What did you have in mind?"

"I could pay you in diamonds," Mr. Teel said.

Everybody around the fire leaned forward at the same instant. A tin plate slid off the major's lap and rattled to the ground.

"Did I hear right? Diamonds?" the major asked.

The stout farmer bristled. "Yes, you did. Is there any

law against a man carrying diamonds?"

"So far as I know," the major answered gruffly, "the law says a man can carry anything he wants to, provided he's come by it honestly. I've seen a lot of things used for money, and that's a fact. Beaver pelts and blankets and gold dust. But if you don't mind my asking, how do you happen to be toting diamonds on the Santa Fe Trail?"

Danny had been itching to ask this same question. Here was a man headed east in a wagon that had a false bottom —traveling away from Santa Fe where a robber had recently stolen jewels from the home of a wealthy Mexican rancher. The robber still hadn't been caught, according to what the stage drivers said. Was this stubborn, slow-moving Pennsylvania farmer really a daring outlaw? If so, what Danny and Flint had done this afternoon was, accidentally, to save the life of a desperate criminal.

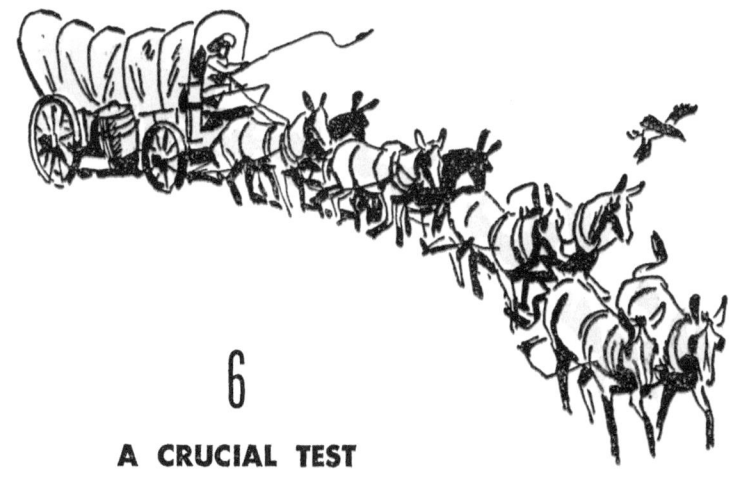

6

A CRUCIAL TEST

Mr. Teel looked sourly at the major. "One thing I always heard about the West—people out here aren't supposed to pry into other people's business."

"No need to get all riled up," Major Adams answered. "I can see why you might take exception to questions about things that were nobody's business but your own. I admit it would make me as cross as a b'ar with two cubs and a sore tail if anybody was to quiz me."

For a few moments the only sound that broke the heavy silence was the fierce snapping of the pitch in a piñon pine knot on the fire. In that short time a conviction swelled up inside Danny with almost explosive force, and he had to let it out somewhere or burst:

"I'll bet anything that man Teel is the outlaw who's wanted for the robbery in Santa Fe," he said in a low voice to Flint, who squatted next to him in the dusk.

"Something about him smells kind of tall, no doubt about that," Flint replied almost in a whisper. "On the other hand, I can't picture him pulling off a big slick robbery, quick and quiet, and getting away without being noticed."

There was a rustle, then a patter of feet behind Danny. He turned and saw Buzz and Bizz running toward their father's wagon. Obviously the twins had been eavesdropping for all they were worth.

The major shifted around and looked squarely at Mr. Teel. "By the way, while you were on the road, did you happen to hear anything about the fellow who stole some diamonds and things in Santa Fe the other day? He hasn't been caught yet."

"Are you accusing me?" the man blustered.

"I'm not accusing anybody. I'm asking a civil question. And I don't mind pointing out that it's a natural question to ask. And it's not prying into anybody's private affairs—unless they need prying into."

"If you don't mind, sir," Colonel Cluggage addressed himself to Mr. Teel, speaking in his soft southern drawl, "I agree with the major. I think you owe it to us to explain. You're asking me to accept diamonds as pay for my mules. But in view of what Major Adams has said, I think I have a right to be sure I'm not accepting stolen diamonds."

The man spluttered, started to say something, stopped, and spluttered again. He seemed confused, and by the time he had recovered from his confusion, Asa Gower had stalked up to the campfire. Behind him in twos and threes hurried the rest of the men in the party. The twins had done a thorough job of spreading the rumor that Flint and Danny thought this stranger was a dangerous outlaw.

Now forty pairs of eyes stared intently at the Pennsylvania farmer who carried diamonds hidden in the false bottom of his Conestoga. And for the second time that day Danny saw terror on the round, bearded face. Earlier he had been surrounded by dark-skinned warriors on horseback who threatened his life. Now white men surrounded him, and they seemed to frighten him even more than the Indians, although they had made no threatening moves as yet.

"Stranger," said Asa Gower presently, "there's things being said about you and diamonds that I don't rightly understand. I sold you a mule. Not much good but the best I had. It seems only fair that I should get honest payment in return."

"That's right, Asa!" shouted another man in the crowd.

"Make him prove he ain't a thief!"

"Make him prove they're real diamonds!" The demand came from Jack the Jug, who waved a bottle in the air.

The hubbub grew, and Danny felt sure some of the men would like nothing better than a chance to beat Teel within an inch of his life, just on general principles. The Pennsylvanian hadn't hurt a soul in this crowd, and yet there were suddenly men here ready to kill him—men who would think they were doing right.

"String him up! Hang the outlaw!" cried the wagoner. He had plainly been drinking too much of the whisky from his bottle.

"Take it easy! Take it easy!" Major Adams shouted, standing up for the first time. But if the crowd heard him they didn't show it. An ugly rumble came from all directions. Now the major moved with the unbelievable speed Danny had seen in him once or twice before. He snatched the whip from the wagon just behind him and sent its twenty-foot length writhing into the darkness. The men in front of him winced, as if each one of them expected to feel the bite of the whip's cracker. The sharp report of it overhead shocked them all into silence. Not a soul made a sound.

"Indians—right here, today—ambushed this man's wagon. They jumped out of nowhere and went after him," the major said in a quiet voice. "For no reason at all, you men are ready to jump him again. You think he robbed somebody in Santa Fe. You know blamed well he didn't rob you. And you don't know whether he robbed anybody. And even if he did, it's not your job to set yourselves up as judges." The major paused. Nobody said a word. "The fact is, Mr. Teel has suggested a business arrangement that's quite a bit out of the ordinary. Since he's asking for our help, and we're willing to give it, I see no harm in asking him to give us a little explanation of the kind of pay he's offering us. And there's one thing I want every man here to see. I'm not putting this whip down. I'll use it on the first hothead who lays a finger on Mr. Teel, no matter how he explains his diamonds."

"Well said, Major Adams!" Colonel Cluggage exclaimed. "Let's hear what Mr. Teel has to say for himself."

Slowly, unsteadily, the bearded Pennsylvanian, who had been frightened limp by the threatening anger of the crowd, now rose and took a step closer to the major, as if for protection. "I didn't steal my diamonds," he blurted out. "I don't know anything about any robbery in Santa Fe."

"Where did you get 'em, then?" Asa Gower asked.

"I dug 'em up myself. I—mined 'em."

"Mined 'em where?"

Unconsciously Danny edged closer to hear Mr. Teel's answer to the question.

"Not very far from here."

Whistles and murmurs of astonishment rose up.

"Mr. Teel," the major said in a firm voice, "I've given

my word that no harm will come to you no matter what you say. And I'll keep it. But this I have to tell you: Most of these men don't know the mountains. I do. There are no diamonds to be mined here. I've guided real experts—geologists—up and down the Rockies, and they say diamonds don't grow here."

The crowd muttered angrily again. "String him up!" yelled Jack the Jug.

Danny turned to Flint. "What did the major want to say that for? He's just stirring everybody up all over again!"

"Don't worry about the major. He'll handle them."

Mr. Teel spoke again. "I don't know anything about geologists. I just know where I found these diamonds. And there's lots more there."

"Hey!" someone called out. "*What* diamonds? Has anybody here seen 'em?"

"I have!" a shrill little voice piped up. It was Buzz, who stood holding his father's hand. "They don't look like much."

"They do too!" his sister cried.

Danny chuckled, looking at Asa Gower whose earnest

face was covered with embarrassment.

"What are those kids talking about?" Flint said to Danny.

"Diamonds," Danny answered. "I saw them too." Then he looked at Mr. Teel whose expression was one of complete amazement.

"Why—why—" he began, and then his manner became that of the threatener rather than the threatened. "If those brats have been snooping around my wagon, stealing my diamonds—"

"Oh, we put them back," Bizz said. "If we'd known they were diamonds, we wouldn't have taken them at all."

"Come on, Mr. Teel," the major said in a businesslike way, "let's see them. The rest of you wait here."

He led the man off toward the big Conestoga, and in a few minutes the two of them returned.

As they approached the fire, Jack the Jug called, "Jush a minute. Anybody here know a real diamond when he sees it?"

The major reached out and took the bottle from the man's hand. "I do!" he answered.

"I think I know a real diamond when I see one," Colonel Cluggage added.

The major squatted beside the fire.

"You can't be sure in that light!" Asa Gower protested.

"I can be sure in the pitch dark," the major answered confidently.

"How?" yelled Jack.

"Give me one of your diamonds, Mr. Teel." The major waited till he held between thumb and forefinger something that Danny couldn't see. "If this is a real diamond it should cut a hole through this glass bottle. . . . It's a wonder the Taos Lightning inside it hasn't already done so," the major added. The crowd laughed.

With hard, steady pressure, the major made a scratch all the way around the base of the whisky bottle. Then he held the bottle in the air and gave the base a smart whack. The bottom dropped away in one smooth piece as if it had been cut by shears. Its owner let out a bellow of despair as the contents spilled on the ground.

A roar of surprised laughter and approval went up. But a moment later Colonel Cluggage had a word to say. "I wish I could agree that you've proved this little stone is a diamond. You played a neat trick on Boozey-Woozey here, but if I'm not mistaken, a sharp piece of quartz will cut glass too. Perhaps this is a quartz crystal you used. However, there is another test we can try, I believe. If we can find a piece of quartz—and if this really is a diamond— then the diamond will scratch the quartz. Does anyone here know what quartz looks like?"

"I do!" Danny said eagerly. He snatched the knobby piñon stick that still blazed in the fire, and, using it for a torch, he ran to inspect the bed of the little stream. In a moment he found a rounded stone of the kind he was looking for. The major and the colonel examined it and agreed it was quartz.

"Hold it so everybody can see it, Danny," the colonel said. "Anybody else want to look it over?"

"It's quartz, all right," several men agreed.

"Now, if the major can make a scratch on it, Mr. Teel certainly has diamonds," the colonel announced.

Danny held the stone ready while the major pressed heavily against it with the tiny object in his fingers. In the flickering light of the fire, he saw a white line appear on the pebble.

There could be no doubt now. Mr. Teel's pouch held real diamonds.

7

DIAMOND TROUBLE

The circle of men pressed closer toward the fire where Major Adams squatted with Danny. Danny looked up, and in the flickering light he saw on every face an intense eagerness to hear the major give his verdict. Not a man in the crowd but had come west in search of fortune. Diamonds stood for riches even more than gold, and right here in their midst might be diamonds.

The major stood up and handed the little crystal back to Mr. Teel. "Beats me where this came from," he said, "but it's a diamond all right."

Men jostled closer, exclaiming, "Let's have a look. . . . Where'd you get it?"

Mr. Teel puffed out angrily. "I told you where it came from—my mine! Are you calling me a liar, Major?"

"I'm not calling you anything, Mr. Teel," Major Adams answered. "I just want to remind you that we found you this afternoon, headed east, away from Santa Fe, and your story was that you'd dropped out of a wagon train because you didn't like the West and wanted to go home. That didn't sound like you'd been mining."

"Major, if you'd found a diamond mine, would you announce it to every Tom, Dick, and Harry that came along?" Mr. Teel asked.

A murmur came from the crowd. This made sense. Naturally a man would be secretive about a mine until he was sure he could protect his interests.

"He has a point there, Major," one man who was a dry-goods merchant said.

"He has a point, but does he have a mine? And if he doesn't have a mine, maybe he's the robber from Santa Fe," Colonel Cluggage said quietly.

Mr. Teel looked frightened anew.

But before he could answer, Jack the Jug shouted, "Robber? Robber, you say? Well, if he's a robber, string him up right now!"

"Shut up! . . . Get along with you! . . . Give Teel a chance to explain!" several men called out at once.

"Jack is right. Do you want to travel along with a bloody outlaw?" a man named Lee came back at them.

Speaking with emotion, Colonel Cluggage answered the questions: "Of course we don't want to travel with an outlaw. But we won't have to, if the man has a mine, as he claims to have."

"The colonel is right," said a man who had been in the hardware business. "Let's not jump to conclusions hastily. I can see Mr. Teel's reasons for telling us a yarn about his desire to go back East. Perhaps if he told us some more about his real reasons for being alone on the trail—"

"Yep! Where were you going?" asked Lee.

"What were you doing on the trail?"

"It's none of your business, but I'll tell you," the burly Pennsylvania farmer said gruffly. "And if it ain't the truth you can cut me up for fish bait. I was heading for Independence—maybe even St. Louis. You see, I've got too big a thing just to handle it with a pick and shovel. I need real mining equipment. I was going to buy me some machinery and I was going to pay for it in diamonds. Everything would have been all right if it hadn't been for those Ute varmints starting to massacree me this afternoon."

"Massacree him! That's the stuff! Let's massacree the outlaw!" Jack the Jug began again to talk up a lynching. This time there was a quick protest. The men were interested in Mr. Teel's fascinating story.

"Gentlemen," Colonel Cluggage said, still in his soft southern drawl, "this is the way I see it. Our leader, Major Adams, says there are no diamonds in these mountains. I myself have always heard that the Rockies are not diamond-iferous. On the other hand, Mr. Teel says he *has* found diamonds—lots of them. And he certainly has a pouch full of them. That much we know. Now there is a way he can prove he came by those diamonds honestly. There's a way he can prove he's a man we can safely travel with."

"How's that?" the dry-goods merchant asked skeptically.

"If we saw the mine ourselves, we'd know," Colonel Cluggage answered.

Mr. Teel let out a bellow of indignation. "And have all of you jumping my claim? No, sirree-bob!"

"I quite agree, sir," the colonel said. "But I have a suggestion. All of us trust our leader, Major Adams. If he saw your mine and told us you really had located diamonds, we would believe him. We would take your diamonds in pay for the mules, and you would be welcome in our train. Am I right?" He threw the question to the crowd.

A cheer went up from the tense listeners.

Danny looked at his employer with real interest. The colonel certainly had a head on his shoulders! Danny had seen so little of him up to now that he hadn't formed any clear picture of what kind of man he was working for.

The colonel turned to Mr. Teel. "Does that strike you as a reasonable proposal, sir?"

"I still don't see why I have to show you anything," Mr. Teel answered.

"You don't *have* to," the colonel replied, and there was an edge to his voice underneath the quiet politeness. "We don't *have* to sell you mules, or take you in, either."

But before Mr. Teel could reply, Major Adams interrupted, pushing his hat back from his forehead the way he always did when he was angry or had something important to say. "This is a bunch of tomfoolishness! I don't know where that so-called mine is supposed to be. But just pretending to look for it would make us lose a day at the very least. I'm responsible for getting this train to Santa Fe on schedule. We already lost time back on the other side of the pass when that young squirt sneaked his train by us. And let me remind you of one more thing. These hills are full of Utes. You saw what they tried to do to Mr. Teel today. I don't know how you all feel about keeping your hair. I like mine—what there is left of it."

A desperado in the wagon train or the possibility of a Ute attack—which was worse? Danny's spine tingled and it tingled again in the silence that followed the major's speech—a silence broken only by the distant, eerie wail of a coyote.

Angrily the major swatted a mosquito that had landed on his forehead, and without saying anything more he waited for a reply.

Mr. Teel brightened up visibly. It seemed to occur to him

that the men in the train were debating dismal alternatives. "I want to be reasonable," he said. "If the major and one other good man will come along to protect me from the Utes, I'll take them up to my mine. It's no more than half a day's ride." He nodded toward the hills on the western side. "We'll be back before dark tomorrow. That way you'll only lose a day."

A hot discussion started now. Danny saw the eyes of the men turning again and again to Mr. Teel's buckskin pouch while they talked. Plenty of them seemed to feel that no matter what the major said, they would find out whether Mr. Teel really was telling the truth. Every man in the party seemed to be thinking, "If Teel has found diamonds, I can too. I can stake out a claim of my own and make my own pile."

A movement on the edge of the crowd caught Danny's attention. Two men were backing away from the circle. What were they up to? he wondered. He eased himself a little farther away from the fire and watched the gray figures leaving the shadow of the willow trees nearby and emerging into a patch of silvery moonlight. Now Danny could tell who they were—two youngish fellows, brothers, by the name of Lee who drove the two extra freight wagons that belonged to the dry-goods merchant. They had been much interested in the diamonds and the discussion. Why were they leaving now when everyone else was so excited? Danny edged along after them.

The two men approached Mr. Teel's wagon. "They're going to look in that hidden compartment," Danny told himself. His heart thumped hard at the thought that he might be witness to a robber being robbed.

But the men didn't even raise the cover of the big Conestoga to look inside. Instead, they studied the ground behind it, and walking slowly about four feet apart, their eyes on the moonlit surface of the hard earth, they withdrew from the clearing.

What could they be doing? Suddenly Danny had the answer. They must be following the tracks left by that Conestoga's wheels! Now they were disappearing in the canyon. Mr. Teel must have come from that direction. The two brothers seemed to be getting pretty strong evidence that Mr. Teel had *not* come from the direction of

Santa Fe. He had come down out of the hills, just as he had indicated when he nodded toward the location of his mine.

The sound of the major's voice brought Danny back to the circle. "Friends," he said, "I think I've got a good idea how you all feel. If there are diamonds, you hate to miss a chance of getting them. I don't blame you. But I'm going to cut this short. I'm in command of this train. We're leaving tomorrow morning on schedule. It's late. You'd better turn in."

This was advice that Danny knew he at least ought to take. It was only a couple of hours till midnight when he would be wakened to stand guard.

Half the men in the train were still muttering and grumbling when Danny crawled out from under the *Poor Richard* at twelve o'clock. By four, however, the camp was quiet, until the customary revolver shot signaled the beginning of a new day.

"Hi, Danny!" Caleb squawked from the top of the *Poor Richard* as Danny approached camp. "Hi, Danny! Wake, snake. Day's a-breakin'."

"Hi, Caleb," Danny replied in the best of moods. He

walked on toward the breakfast fire, well satisfied with himself. Yes, indeed. He had been less jittery last night than the first time he did guard duty. He could even poke a little fun at himself for what he had done on that unhappy occasion.

"Didn't see a single mule to shoot at last night," he complained to Flint.

But Flint seemed preoccupied, worried about something. At this hour of the day he was usually full of high spirits, jollying the drivers and others along and doing everything he could to speed up departure.

"What's the matter, Flint?" Danny asked.

"Plenty!" Flint jerked a thumb toward the wagon called *Mind Your Own Business*. "Take a look."

The sun hadn't come up, but there was enough light to show Danny what Flint meant. Underneath other wagons were buffalo robes or blankets as usual, rumpled and heaped where occupants had been sleeping. But there was nothing under *Mind Your Own Business*. The Lee brothers hadn't slept there last night!

The brothers! Suddenly Danny remembered the scene

in the moonlight. He had seen the two men following the tracks left by Mr. Teel's wagon. They were headed up the canyon. Had something happened to them up there? Danny had heard no shots, but an arrow was silent. He himself had pulled arrows out of Mr. Teel's wagon yesterday. With awful certainty he said to himself, "Those men are dead! And they'd be alive right now except for me. I should have thought to warn Flint or the major when I saw them leaving camp!"

8

SMOKE SIGNALS!

There was no doubt about it, the Lee brothers had disappeared. Nobody, not even Buzz and Bizz, had seen them since last evening. And the major was furious.

Flint poked Danny and said, "You've never seen the major when he was mad, have you?"

Danny was surprised at the look on Flint's face. He seemed to be anticipating something with pleasure, in spite of the seriousness of the situation. "Sure, the major's been mad plenty of times."

"But you haven't seen him when he was on a real rampoose," Flint declared softly. "Lay low now, and hold your breath. The major's about to turn himself loose."

The major did. "Some of you men are tickled pink because I have to go look for those Lee boys. It doesn't worry you that they might be dead. All you care is that you've got me where you want me. We can't move out of here, because the two Lees tried to sneak off and pocket a few diamonds before anybody else gets a chance. All right. If I find those two anywhere handy—and if I've got any breath left after I tell 'em what I think of 'em—I'll go on with Teel and take a look at what he claims is his diamond mine. The rest of you will stay here. Flint McCullough will be in charge. He has orders to shoot any omnigenous gumbo-limbo, copper-bellied, cityfied muleycow that tries to wander out of this corral. He'll ramsquaddle the whole lot of you if he has to." The major paused for breath. "Now I need one more man to go along with Mr. Teel and me. And there's only one of you that's got half the sense that God promised a grown man. Danny, saddle up and bring your rifle."

Danny had been so absorbed in the major's "rampoose" that he didn't get the full significance of the order for a moment. Then he realized that the major was saying he trusted Danny more than any of the forty men in the train.

This thought frightened Danny. He had a terrible responsibility now. On top of that he had an awful feeling that he himself had caused the trouble in the first place. The major didn't know this, of course. He didn't know that Danny had failed to report the activity of the Lee brothers last night. But there was one good thing about the major's decision to take him along. It gave him a chance to make amends for his mistake.

Danny went to saddle horses for himself, the major, Mr. Teel, and for the two Lees if and when they were located. As he worked, he kept wishing everything would work out all right. He hoped he would never have to explain to the major about last night.

Riding along the trail that morning was grim business from the very start. At the entrance to the canyon Caleb turned up to worry Danny. He swooped down, screeching, "Ah-whooh-wah!" Mr. Teel jumped. The major, too, was surprised. He looked around, obviously startled at hearing the cry of a stagecoach driver up here away from the trail. He hadn't yet descended from his fine pinnacle of rage, and Danny expected Caleb's behavior to set off more trouble.

Vainly Danny tried to shoo the crow back to the wagon circle. But the major was feeling so ornery this morning that he seemed to get a kind of satisfaction out of having the bird around. Although he didn't have a word to say to Mr. Teel or Danny as he rode along, he began talking to the crow.

"Caleb, no doubt about it, those cussed Lee brothers are trying to trace Mr. Teel's wagon back to his cockeyed, so-called diamond mine."

A little later, he added, "Caleb, in case those fellows don't know it, they're likely to walk into a big Ute encampment. There must be pretty considerable much of a Ute gathering going on, from the looks of the hoofprints along this trail."

Danny took a sharp look at the ground. The major was right. Dozens of horsemen must have passed this way recently!

"Caleb, it would be nice to know what kind of taffy pull those Utes are having," the major said thoughtfully. "Maybe the twin chiefs told me the truth and they're getting together to go on a buffalo hunt. On the other hand, they

might be fixing to bust loose the way they did last year.
I sure hope the Lee boys don't do some idiot thing that will
make them mad."

"Holy Moses!" was the crow's comment.

"And another thing, Caleb. I'm going to give those Lees
a sizable piece of thinking to do when we meet up with
them. I'm going to ask them to figure out how I'll ever
persuade old Kanneatche and Curicata that I was speaking
the truth when I told them I would take my wagon train
right through their country. I'm going to ask the Lees why
those Ute chiefs shouldn't scalp me for a liar. You know,
Caleb, I've heard tell that's what the Utes do to people who
break their word. I gave my solemn promise that this
train wouldn't cause the Utes any trouble. But here my
wagons are, camped right on a Ute trail. And here I am
looking for a mine on Ute land. If there's one thing a Ute
likes less than another it's a miner, because when prospectors move in, game moves out."

As the major's speech went on, Mr. Teel grew more and
more nervous. Danny himself certainly felt ill at ease, and
what happened next threw him into a momentary panic.

"Drop your guns!" a voice ordered. "I've got you covered."

"Drop 'em!" another voice called.

It was a moment before Danny realized that the orders were coming from the Lee brothers, hiding behind a big boulder. He clung to his rifle, his arms stiff with fear. He couldn't drop it, or aim it either. As if from a great distance he heard the major thundering out, "You chicken-livered, gutter-sniping nincompoops! Come to your senses. Put that six-shooter away and come here. I know you've only got that one shooting iron between the two of you. I checked your wagon. You left the other one there. There's three of us. So the odds are against you. Besides, your hand's shaking so you couldn't hit the side of a blind old bull buffalo if he was trying to scratch himself on that rock you're hiding behind."

Looking exceedingly limp, the fat Lee came around the edge of the rock. Even his revolver looked limp, Danny thought.

"Give me that thing," the major ordered. "It might go off accidentally and hurt you. I've come this far after you,

and I'd hate to take you back all messy. The simple, gol-blamed truth is, I hate to take you back at all. You two look just like the type that makes a habit of stealing candy from little kids and feeling smart about it. Well, the joke's on you. If there are any diamonds to be found, you're going to watch me and Danny find them. Now get on these horses we brought you out of the everlasting kindness of our hearts, and ride ahead of us. And don't try any surprises." He tapped his rifle and his Colt significantly.

"By the way," the major added as they started on, "you fellows look like a pretty poor excuse for road agents. Just what did you have in mind when you had that six-shooter pointed at me?"

The fat Lee, who sat in the saddle like a balloon with half the air gone out of it, replied, "We were afraid you wouldn't let us finish our hunt for the diamond mine. So we figured we'd make you go along with us. We didn't mean any harm."

Danny had been up most of the night, and soon he was feeling mildly cranky. Whether the major had slept at all was doubtful, and cranky was not the word to describe him! But the Lees, neither of whom looked athletic, must be just plain petered out, Danny thought to himself. They had been up all night, walking, through Indian country, straining hard to follow wagon tracks by the dim light of the moon. Besides, they hadn't even had any sowbelly and beans to fortify them for the day. Trouble with these two might not be over.

The farther they went up the canyon, the more nervous Mr. Teel seemed to be growing. Danny wasn't surprised. They were following a Ute trail, and only yesterday the Utes had given the big man a bad time. Even the major began to notice something peculiar. Mr. Teel rode closer and closer to the wagon train master, as if being near him would somehow guarantee his own safety.

Finally the major drew rein and stared for a long time at the story that was told by tracks in the hard-baked clay of the canyon floor. Even Danny, who was a novice at following tracks, could see what had happened here, although he couldn't guess *why* it had happened. The marks left by the iron wagon tires continued in the canyon bottom. But the Indian horse trail, much used, turned sharply up the slope to the right. There seemed to be no hoofprints left by Ute ponies going in the direction of the wheel tracks. What did this mean?

The major, too, seemed curious. A little farther along he chose a good shady spot in which to rest the horses and ask some pertinent questions.

"Mr. Teel, do you mind telling me how you happened to be up here by yourself in Indian country looking for diamonds—which you couldn't have heard were here, because nobody else ever heard it?"

It was plain that the major still had to be convinced there was a diamond deposit in the Rocky Mountains.

"Oh, I wasn't looking for diamonds," Mr. Teel answered. He seemed a little surprised at the major's questions. "I was looking for gold. I did a little panning the first part of the summer when I came out from the East. The train I was with made camp right where you're camped now. The creek was big then, and I panned there and got a showing of gold. So I dropped out of the train and went prospecting seriously."

Danny interrupted. "Why did they let you drop out?"

"The wagon master wasn't exactly like Major Adams. He said it was my own funeral."

"That sounds like Pokey Smith," the major remarked.

Teel gave a giggle. "Pokey—that's who it was. At any rate, I worked my way up the creek a little bit farther every day. Didn't even get enough gold dust to make you sneeze, and I was just about to clear out when I ran into this diamond field."

The major looked at him sharply. "Are you a gem expert or something, so you know diamonds when you find them growing wild?"

"No, sir. The only diamonds I ever saw before were in a jewelry store window in Pittsburgh. I wasn't sure I had 'em at first. I just had a funny feeling—a hunch. You know how it is?"

The major nodded. "Mebbe. I hear that prospectors get hunches all the time, but I ain't seen many of them get rich. Personally, if you want my opinion, a hunch ain't worth shucks. Sweat and calluses will get you a lot farther. But tell me, how did you find out for sure you had located diamonds? The nearest diamond assaying office is in Africa somewhere, I should think. Isn't that right?"

"I got the stagecoach to take a parcel to a geologist in Santa Fe. I put some of the rocks in the parcel, and then I waited for the stage driver to bring me back my answer."

"Hmm," the major said. Then after a moment, "You were up this canyon all summer long, and the Utes never bothered you till yesterday." A canny expression crossed his face.

"How could they bother me? There weren't any of them around here, so far as I know, until a couple of days ago. As soon as I saw them, I decided the time was just ripe for me to head east and get my mining machinery."

"Well, that was sensible," the major said. "I think you ought to know that I'm not at all sure it was Utes who ambushed you yesterday."

The eyes bugged out of Mr. Teel's round face. "I—I— saw 'em!" he said.

"Oh, I'm not trying to call you a liar, or crazy, or anything like that. What I mean is this: I've never heard of a Ute that shot a mule or a horse when he could steal it. Stealing horses is honorable work among the Utes. I mean that.

The best horse thief is the most respected man in his band."

Mr. Teel stammered out again, "But I saw 'em."

"Just let me finish, and you'll feel better. There are quite a few white-skinned varmints along this trail that dress up like Utes and make a good living robbing wagon trains and stagecoaches. The Utes get the blame and the outlaws get the loot. I'd be willing to bet that you ran into a gang of road agents decked out like Utes."

The major paused, then returned to the purpose of the expedition. "How much farther do we have to go?" he asked.

"We'll be there in a few minutes," Mr. Teel answered.

The party started on. Caleb had been taking his ease, perched on Tennessee's rump. When the horse stirred, the crow flapped into the air, uttering a loud protest at being disturbed. Danny looked up and waved an arm at his pet, inviting him to come down and ride if he was too lazy to fly. In the moment when his eyes were cast upward, Danny saw something peculiar against the ridge far above. He looked a second time. A column of smoke was rising almost straight up in the calm midmorning air, but suddenly it seemed to be cut off at the bottom. Then smoke came in puffs—one, two, three, Danny counted. And one, two, three again.

"Major!" Danny called. "Look! Smoke signals!"

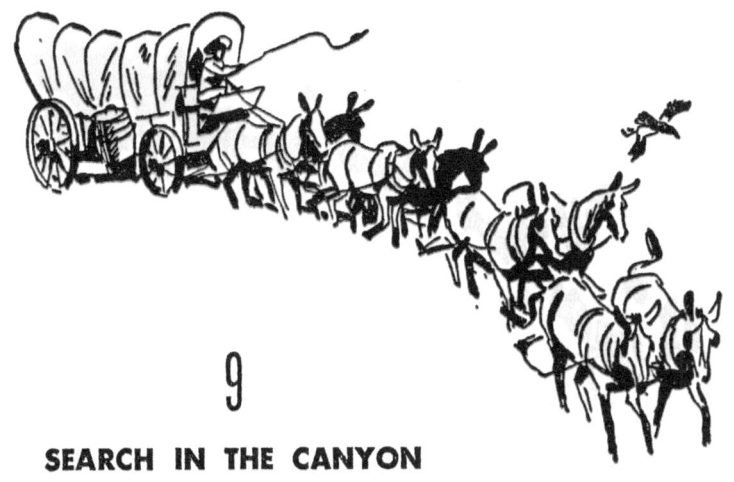

9

SEARCH IN THE CANYON

"How many did you count, Danny?" the major asked.

"Three and then three more, I think."

"Well, that's a warning in smoke signal language."

"How in thunder are we supposed to know that?" the fat Lee brother demanded.

"They're not warning *us*," the major answered scornfully, "although we might be smart to take the hint. They're warning each other that some white men are trespassing on their real estate."

"Maybe—maybe we'd better forget the diamonds," the tall Lee suggested.

"A fine time to say that!" the major jeered. "After getting us into this everlasting fix, you want to back out of it before it does anybody any good! I'm going to take time enough now to settle this diamond business if it's the last thing I do." He looked at the brother maliciously. "And while I dig for diamonds I'm going to station one of you on one side of me and the other on the other side—to stop any Ute arrows that might come my way."

The fat Lee looked green but said nothing. After all, there wasn't much he could say. In silence they all rode on into an open spot where the canyon widened and the bottom was covered with several acres of gravel and sand, in which only an occasional random patch of grass had managed to take root.

In a grove of pines on the far side, Danny saw signs of the camp that Mr. Teel had made there. Toward the middle of the flat area rose a mound of gravel. Beside it was a large shallow pit.

"Here we are! You can dig wherever you want to, Major. But I found the diamonds were thickest about a foot down, right on top of a bed of clay."

A minute later Mr. Teel had brought a pick and shovel

and a ratty-looking buffalo skin from a hiding place near the pines. Meantime Danny dismounted and studied the pit intently. It was perhaps forty feet long and ten feet wide. For about half of its length it was nearly a foot deep, with a clay bottom. The other half Mr. Teel had obviously not finished working when he decided to leave. Danny could see why the man would want to get machinery in to help him with the job. It would be terrific labor to shovel and sift all the heavy gravel around here.

"You can work it any way you please," Mr. Teel said to the major. "But this is how I do it. I shovel out the stuff onto this old buffalo hide. Then I sort it over by hand and dump it onto the waste pile."

The major thought a minute. Then he said to the Lee brothers, "You two jump down into the hole. Start shoveling over at this end where Teel left off. Heave the gravel onto the buffalo hide, like the feller says. Danny, you look the stuff over. I'm going to keep my eye on things."

"Mr. Teel, where do you think we ought to dig?" the fat Lee asked.

"Diamonds are where you find 'em," was the answer.

"They are probably in the layer underneath the clay too, but I haven't looked there yet. Most of the ones I've found are between six and twelve inches down."

The fat Lee began to loosen the gravel with the pick, and the lean one heaved it up onto the buffalo hide. Danny, on his knees, moved the stuff toward him a little at a time. It was going to be slow work, but it seemed the only way to look for small, glossy pebbles like those he had seen in the pouch.

Danny had gone through three shovelfuls and was beginning to grow very bored with his task when a glint of light came from the dull gray and tan heap in front of him. "Hey, Major! I think I've got one!" he cried.

The Lees dropped pick and shovel. "Let's see!" the fat one croaked. His excitement was so great that his voice almost failed him.

The tall one jumped out of the pit and fell to his hands and knees on the gravel heap like a bloodhound sniffing its quarry. "Where is it?"

"Back up," Danny answered, "and I'll show you."

Grudgingly the man moved his lanky frame back, so

that full sunlight fell on the gravel heap. Danny pointed to the glinting pebble. The Lees reached toward it.

"Hold on!" the major barked. "Get out of the way. Let me have a look at this so-called diamond." It was his turn now to get down on all fours. He picked up the shiny bit. "Looks to me like a chunk of glass," he said. After turning it around between thumb and forefinger, he rose to his feet. "The rest of you keep on working."

The major stepped back from the heap of gravel on the buffalo hide. But before he did anything else he took a careful look at the hillsides all around. Plainly he didn't intend to let anything interfere with his determination to keep an eye out for Indians. Then he walked downstream a little way, and in a moment Danny saw what he was doing. He stooped, picked up a white rock—quartz, of course —and scratched at it. Forgetting the search, Danny and the Lees waited. They didn't have to ask what the result was.

The major's face told them. The little bit of shiny crystal was, indeed, a diamond. In some other place, and at some other time, Major Adams would have been as excited as anyone else by such a discovery. But right now, here in this country, with his wagon train already late, a real diamond was the last thing in the world he wanted to find.

"It don't seem natural, and I can't make it out," he said, shaking his head. "There *aren't* any diamonds in the Rocky Mountains."

Feverishly now the fat Lee began to heave gravel up onto the buffalo hide.

"Take it easy!" Danny cried cheerfully. "You're covering me up. Give me a chance to hunt."

Without asking the major's permission, both of the brothers stopped their work and knelt beside Danny. Soon the fat one burst out, "Lookit! A diamond!" He held up a tiny crystal.

"I guess that does it," the major said with a resigned air. "There are diamonds here, all right. Let's go."

"Hey, give *me* a chance," the other Lee protested. "I haven't got one yet. I want me a diamond too."

"Let me tell you a secret, Sugar Cane," the major said. "Butterball here hasn't *got* a diamond and neither has Danny. Those things belong to Mr. Teel. It's his mine."

With a smile Mr. Teel held out his hand for the diamonds

that Danny and the Lee brother had to agree were his. "Why don't you look a little bit farther, Major, just to make doubly sure?"

The major hesitated. "Maybe you're right, Teel. I'm being a mite hasty, I guess. We've come all this way, and I suppose we ought to do a good job of it." He surveyed the whole flat area, considering where to make the next test —obviously in a spot some distance from the pit.

"All right, Danny," the major said in a moment. "You and Sugar Cane dump that stuff into the pit and bring the hide over here. Butterball, bring the pick and shovel."

Danny stood and stretched. He was cramped from being hunkered over on his knees. As he threw back his head, he caught a glint of reflected light from a spot near the ridge to the north. The flash disappeared but there was something moving right where it had been. A sickening suspicion swept over Danny. It was as if his bones had gone soft.

Then suspicion gave way to certainty. A Ute stood, high on the hillside, watching them from a patch of scrub oak. Sunlight had glinted from his rifle as he emerged over the top of the ridge.

Danny tried to collect his thoughts. "I'll pretend I haven't noticed anything," he said to himself, not knowing quite why. Then, trying to look casual, he approached the major and said in a voice so low it would be hard for the others to hear, "I just looked up the hill. We've got a visitor. A Ute is watching us from the ridge behind my back."

The major finished loading the shovel and tossed the gravel aside. Then he leaned on the handle and raised his eyes to the ridge. "You look sharp to the south, Danny, and tell me if you see any others among the trees."

Danny looked hard. "Nobody there," he answered in a little while.

"There's only that one to the north," the major said. "He must be alone. Let's hope he stays that way long enough for us to get out of here."

Danny turned.

"Mr. Teel," the major said, "on second thought, I don't think it's worth the trouble to dig any more. It wouldn't prove anything if we dug all day and didn't find another diamond. It would still be a fact that there *are* diamonds here. Come on. We're leaving."

With exasperating slowness the Lees placed the tools and the folded buffalo hide where Mr. Teel said he wanted them cached. At last Danny and the four men started their horses back down the canyon.

Danny and the major rode side by side. "That was a piece of bad luck," said the major quietly. "I wish that Ute hadn't seen me."

Danny wondered if the major really thought just being seen here would cause a Ute attack. He got his answer when the wagon train master went on, "A lot of numskulls on the train don't seem to remember I gave my word to the twin chiefs that I was going right through their country —not stopping for anything. And here I am, dillydallying, messing around, way off from the Santa Fe Trail."

"Oh, he probably didn't recognize you," Danny said hopefully.

Major Adams snorted. "You don't know the Indians. Maybe this fellow up on the hill doesn't recognize me. But when he gets back to his encampment he'll describe me. He'll say he saw a white man, and then he'll go on with the shape of this old hat of mine, and the exact color of my hair and the way I walk. And the chiefs and any other Ute who has ever seen me will know precisely who was up here breaking a promise today. And then anything might happen."

The major was certainly no coward, and he didn't go around dreaming up dangers that didn't exist. But he was glum right now, very glum indeed. Presently he seemed to decide something. "Let's not make unnecessary trouble for ourselves, Danny," he said. "There's no need to stir things up—for a while, anyway. I'm not going to tell those other galoots that we saw an Indian spying on us, and I hope you won't either. The news might scare Teel and the Lees and make them act as if they were running away. We don't want the Utes to find out that we really *are* scared."

The discovery that the major could be afraid had a curious effect on Danny; that, and the way the older man had confided in him. Instead of becoming more frightened, he felt better. It was a relief to know that he wasn't alone with his fear. The major was with him. Moreover, he had made a suggestion to Danny instead of giving an order— had treated him as if he were a close friend, an equal.

Caleb, who had been riding on the horn of Danny's saddle, flapped up into the air at this point, bored with the silence into which his owner had subsided. For a while the crow glided overhead, riding currents of hot afternoon air that moved up the canyon. Then he swooped off and disappeared in the direction of camp.

Just before the party emerged from the canyon in full view of the wagons, the major called a halt. Facing Danny and the others, he spoke: "I want to warn you all about one thing, and it's more important than I've got time to explain. *Don't any of you tell where the diamond mine is located.* I don't say this just to protect Mr. Teel's property. I want to protect his life and your lives, the lives of everybody. Another visit to that mine might touch off an Indian uprising. The Utes are having a big powwow of some sort up that way. They are galled and sore at the whites for streaming over their land. If we started a diamond rush now, they might butcher the whole lot of us. So, I'll repeat it. I'm not asking you—I'm warning you. Don't tell anybody where the mine is. No matter what, the train is going to roll tomorrow." There was steel in the major's voice.

"Do I have your word?" he demanded with a stern face.

Danny and the others nodded. But the major soon found that it was one thing to plan a start tomorrow morning, and quite another thing to get under way. Things had been happening in camp, things that no one could have foreseen.

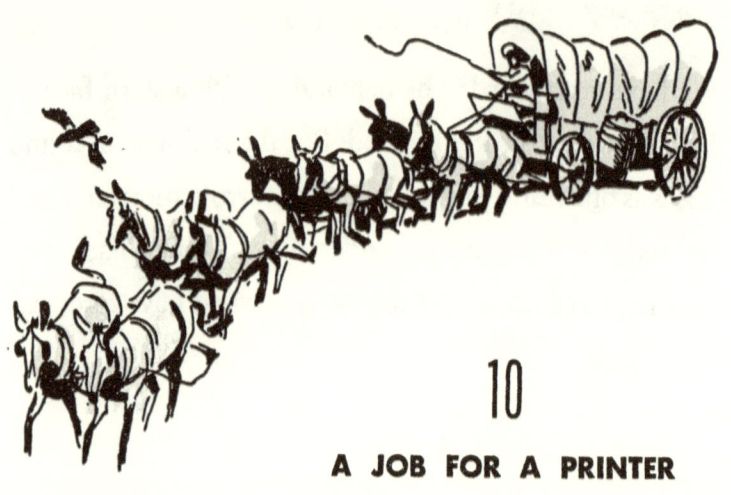

10

A JOB FOR A PRINTER

"It's a good thing you're back, Danny!" This shrill announcement came from Bizz who dashed out from among the wagons to meet the horsemen. "Caleb came home before you did. He made Mamma awful mad!"

"What happened?" Danny asked.

"Mamma washed some clothes and hung them on a line to dry."

Danny grinned. He knew the rest of the story without being told. Back in Independence Caleb had discovered what fun it was to pull a clothespin off the line and fly around with it in his beak. He thoroughly enjoyed the sight of shirts and dresses fluttering to the ground after he plucked a lot of clothespins off. Danny shuddered to think of what had happened to Mrs. Gower's fresh-washed laundry. Except for the trickle of water in the stream, everything within sight was bone dry, and all around the wagon train the ground had been scuffed until the surface had turned into loose, fine, powdery dust.

"I'll speak to Caleb about that," Danny said. "Thanks, anyway, for warning me."

"Holy Moses!" floated down from a treetop near the stream. And then Caleb himself swooped toward Danny and landed on his shoulder.

"Caleb—" Danny began to gather words for a solemn lecture. But the twins interrupted.

"Did you find any diamonds?" Buzz asked.

Before answering, Danny paused and listened to the major, who was addressing the assembled wagon train. A cautious streak in Danny warned him not to give Bizz and Buzz the first hint that there really were diamonds up the canyon.

Major Adams, standing in the rear of his wagon, was just remarking solemnly, "What good is a pocket full of diamonds if you've lost your scalp?"

It was clear that the members of the wagon train had now heard approximately the same speech Danny had heard just a little way out of camp. "Yep, young ones," he said to the twins. "We found diamonds."

"Rats!" Buzz said in disgust. "Mr. Teel isn't an outlaw then. Isn't there *ever* going to be anything interesting in this wagon train?"

"And we'll be almost the only ones that won't get rich," Bizz added dismally.

"Now what do you mean by that?" Danny exclaimed.

"You just ask Colonel Cluggage. He'll tell you."

Puzzled, Danny unsaddled Tennessee, hobbled him, and turned him loose with the other animals in the cavvyard. By the time he returned to the circle of wagons, Colonel Cluggage had appeared at the edge of the crowd, listening to the animated talk between the major and some of the other men. In answer to Danny's question, the colonel said, smiling, "I think I know what the youngsters meant. While you were gone, some of the speculators among us decided to help Mr. Teel, and to do ourselves a good turn at the same time. Provided, of course, that you found diamonds and that Mr. Teel was willing to accept help."

That still didn't make sense, and Danny said so.

"The long and short of it is that we agreed to form a stock company. That means we'll all invest some money in Mr. Teel's mine. He will take the money back East and buy machinery. As I understand it, he will need to build a dam or drill a deep well and then use pressure pumps in order to wash the diamonds out of the gravel."

"He sure does need some kind of machinery," Danny said. "It's an awful job to mine them by hand."

"Well, then," the colonel went on, "everybody who gives Mr. Teel a hundred dollars will get one share of stock. Then when the mine begins to make money, the people who bought the stock will share in the profits. If it is a rich diamond field, all of the stockholders stand to make a pretty penny."

"Oh," said Danny. "I see. I guess I understand what the twins were talking about." He felt quite sure that Mr. Gower didn't have a hundred dollars. It would be a miracle if he had more than ten dollars. Plainly, diamonds were not going to make him a rich man.

But plenty of men in this train did have money. A good many were businessmen traveling by wagon instead of by coach in order to be with the valuable cargoes of merchandise they were moving west.

"And, young man, I have news for you too," the colonel went on. He seemed in high spirits. With a grand gesture he pointed at the *Poor Richard* which stood in the midst of the freight it had been carrying. Almost everything but the printing press was lying on the dusty ground.

"What in the world—" Danny began.

"Even before we get to Santa Fe, we have a chance to start putting that press of ours to good use. The men who want to buy shares in Mr. Teel's mine would feel better if they had regular printed stock as proof they had invested their money."

"How's that again?" Danny asked.

"It is customary," the colonel explained, "for a company to have shares of stock printed up. A share is a piece of paper that tells the name of the company, maybe who the officers of the company are, what the stock is supposed to be worth, and so on. And, of course, a share of the stock is your proof that you have invested money in the company and are entitled to share in the profits. So, since we have the press, and there was nothing to do today, I got everything all ready so that you can set the type if Mr. Teel agrees."

Danny approached the *Poor Richard* with a new interest. All the way across the plains he had been driving a wagon loaded with a printing press that he had never even seen. Now, in the most unexpected place and under unusual circumstances, he was going to have a chance to use it! The big wagon was almost empty, except for the press which was bolted to the wagon floor. It was an old Washington press, just like the one he had always worked on at home, so he would have no difficulty. The colonel had even unpacked the cases of type and the rest of the equipment. Under its canvas top the *Poor Richard* was a tidy workroom. Danny chuckled to himself. This was a sheer delight.

"Do we have the right kind of paper too?" he asked.

"Of course! How can we start a print shop without paper? We've got all kinds," the colonel answered jovially. He indicated rectangular packages of various sizes wrapped in oilskin to keep them clean and dry.

"Well! When do I start?" Danny asked.

"The minute Mr. Teel gives you the order," the colonel answered. "Some of the men wrote up the words they want you to set. They're ready for you as soon as everybody agrees and the officers of the company are elected."

Danny hurried back to the crowd around the major's *Santa Maria.* He hoped that they would decide about the shares of stock right away. He wanted to do as much work as possible by daylight. If necessary he could print by candlelight, although it wasn't very pleasant. But he knew the major would make him rush, so that the wagon train could start on time tomorrow morning. Maybe he would have to be up all night working—and repacking the wagon after the printing was done.

"Of all the sorry, addlepated, muddleheaded, mosquito-brained emigrants I ever led across the plains, you are the sorriest!" the major was saying in a low but intense and penetrating voice. "You'd rather be rich than alive. All right. You win. You've got me between a rock and a hard place. I know when I'm licked. I can't make this wagon train move if nine tenths of the drivers traipse off looking at the diamond mine they've bought a piece of. You can go up there tomorrow morning. But I'm coming along with an extra pick and shovel."

"I expected you'd come to your senses, Major," cried the fat Lee brother. "How much stock are you buying?"

"I'm not buying one wooden nickel's worth. But somebody has to bury you fools when the Utes get through with you."

Danny thought that this might discourage anyone who wanted to go on the expedition tomorrow. But nothing of the sort happened. Mania had seized these men. He was sure they would wade hip-deep through molten lava if they thought they could get quickly to the diamonds that meant riches.

Things began to move fast now. Before long, the Western Diamond Company had been formed and the colonel had sent Danny running to the *Poor Richard* with a handwritten copy of the words he was to set up and print.

Danny found his fingers stiff from the calluses and the big muscles he had developed tugging, day after day, on the reins that controlled eight ornery mules. But, stiff or not, he enjoyed the work from which he had had a change for the last six weeks. Caleb, too, seemed to like the familiar activity of a print shop. He circulated around the tight quarters in the wagon, but most of the time he perched on top of the type cases, repeating over and over again, as if all this were too good to be true, "Hi, Danny! Holy Moses!"

As he worked, taking the letters one by one out of the little compartments in which they were stored, Danny heard bits of the first official meeting of the stockholders in the company.

"I nominate Colonel Cluggage for president," somebody called out.

The colonel declined. Mr. Teel, he said, should be president, because it was Mr. Teel's mine. And so it was voted.

"I want to nominate the treasurer," Danny heard a little later. A voice began to imitate the major: "I want to nominate the man who may be the gol-durndest, grumpiest, most cantankerous wagon master this side of the Mississippi—as I say, he may be ornery, but he's honest. Major Adams for treasurer."

There was a cheer, followed by a large and heartfelt growl from the major. "No!"

The next Danny heard, Colonel Cluggage was nominated. The colonel made a speech, ending, "And so I accept on one condition. I'll keep track of the money, if the major will consent to hold it for us until we can put it in the bank in Santa Fe."

"Hold it yourself," the major snarled. But out of the confused arguments that followed, Danny guessed that the major at last agreed to keep the money in the strongbox he carried in his wagon.

"Whew-ee!" came a voice from the opening in the canvas that covered the impromptu print shop. It was Flint. "I've seen some emigrants go wild when they met their first buffalo herd. I've seen 'em go wild at the mention of gold. But diamonds! Diamonds beat them all."

Danny laughed and went on setting type while Flint watched his fingers flying back and forth, picking out the tiny letters and putting them into position accurately.

"Say! You know what you're doing, all right!" Flint said with admiration.

When, a minute or two later, Major Adams came by, Flint was ready to show Danny off as if he had personally invented him. "Look at that, Major! Did you know what we had with us all this time?"

But the major was in no mood to be impressed. He grunted, then said to Flint earnestly, "You know, I've seen a lot of crazy things in my day, but this stock company is the craziest. I've seen honest companies and crooked companies, and honest-crooked and crooked-honest—and this isn't like any of 'em. Usually it's the company that tries to sell the stock. Now here there wasn't even a company until people started fighting to start one, and they're pushing their money onto poor old Teel although he didn't even know he wanted it!"

"Do you think there's something that isn't open and aboveboard?" Flint asked.

"If I thought it was crooked, I would stop it!" the major spluttered. "But it's so blamed honest that I'm holding all the money. I can give it back if I'm a mind to. Nobody's lost anything in this whole deal so far—but time! I just hope nobody loses a scalp," he added. "I'm going with those idiots tomorrow. If they're to have a run-in with the Utes, I want to be on hand. I gave my word to the twin chiefs that we wouldn't stop, and then I had to break it. I have a sneaking suspicion that if I could just have a talk with Kanneatche and Curicata I could make them understand that I'm not a liar. They probably have trouble themselves when men in their band get crazy ideas."

The major went off, still mumbling and grumbling, and Flint followed him.

Suddenly something bumped against Danny's foot.

"Caleb! Can't you keep out of the way?" Danny cried.

The crow could, but he didn't. He rested by turns on top of the type case and the top of the press, but soon he was back waddling and strutting around the floor of the wagon.

Danny's job of typesetting was almost finished. All he needed was the names of the company's officers, spelled out. And these he soon got, by messenger. The twins appeared, and Bizz waved a piece of paper as she ran.

"The colonel told me to give you this," she said. "Are you going to get rich too, Danny?"

"How could I? I haven't got any money to buy stock.

Say, do you kids want to do me a favor?" Danny asked, glancing out through the opening in the wagon. It was still light, and he wanted the benefit of every minute before dark. "Go over and get me a plate of beans and sowbelly from the pot on the major's fire. I'll be ready to start printing in a little while and you can watch me run this big machine here."

"All right, fine," Bizz called over her shoulder.

To let in the last of the daylight, Danny threw back the canvas top. The setting sun struck directly on the case of type, and a glint quite different from that of metal type was reflected from the case. Curious, Danny looked closer. There, mixed in with the capital Q's, was a tiny sparkling thing that at any other time he would have thought was just a piece of broken glass. But today his thoughts ran to diamonds. Was it a diamond? How could it be? Where did it come from? How could a diamond have got mixed in with the type?

11

TRAGEDY IN THE DARK

How *could* a diamond get into his box of type? The answer came to Danny as he stood, bemused, in the midst of his printing equipment. Caleb could have put it there. The saucy crow had been in and out, overhead and underfoot—all over the place. Come to think of it, he had perched several times on top of the type case.

Danny fingered the little gleaming crystal and said aloud, "Where did you get this, you scoundrel?"

"Holy Moses!" was Caleb's only comment.

Danny shook his head and grinned. "Did you steal it from Mr. Teel?"

"Hi, Danny! Holy Moses!"

"Or maybe you got it from the Lee brothers?" Was it possible that one of those two good-for-nothings had picked up a diamond at the mine and managed to keep it a secret? But if so, how did Caleb manage to steal it?

Or maybe somebody had found another diamond field right near by, and Caleb had robbed him. Or maybe Caleb himself had located a new diamond mine! Starting with this last thought Danny could see the future opening out. In no time he would have his own stock printed up. He would sell it. His fortune would be made, and he could splurge around something bodacious!

"Caleb, you fine, noble, devilish little monster! Show me where in the name of Jehoshaphat your diamond mine is!"

"Ah-whooh-wah! Holy Moses!" Caleb screeched, and he flew up onto one of the wagon bows from which Danny had removed the canvas. There he sat with his head cocked, uttering what sounded remarkably like a laugh at Danny's expense: "Haw-haw! Haw-haw!"

The dazzling thought of a mining company of his own made Danny postpone for a few minutes the printing of Mr. Teel's stock. He quickly set up the last of the type and then went to see Mr. Teel in person. The man was stretched out resting on the buffalo robe under his wagon, and he opened his eyes when Danny spoke.

"Howdy. I thought you'd like to know I'm almost ready to print up your stock. I just have to let the thregastus settle a little."

Mr. Teel nodded as if he understood how important this was, and Danny vowed inwardly to remember the word *thregastus*. It had come to him like a beautiful inspiration on the spur of the moment, and it might prove handy plenty of times before he had worn it to a frazzle.

"Do you mind if I ask you a personal question?" Danny went on.

"I guess that depends," Mr. Teel said cautiously.

"It's nothing special. Not like finding out how much money you're going to make from the diamonds you've already got out of the mine or that sort of stuff. I was just wondering how many of them you've dug up."

"And what do you want to know that for?" Mr. Teel sounded suspicious.

"Well, you see, I've got a kind of bet. I made a guess, and

if I'm wrong, I'm going to lose. You know how that is."

"Humph." Mr. Teel relaxed. "Thirty-seven."

"Thirty-seven. That's bad for me. Are you sure?"

"Of course I'm sure."

"Mr. Teel, do me a big favor, will you? Could you count your diamonds again, just to make certain? I had a dream, and a lot depends on that dream coming true."

Mr. Teel was immediately suspicious again. "I thought you said you had a bet."

"Of course. I bet on my dream," Danny said earnestly.

"Now, you look here," the man said. "Are you trying to tell me my diamonds are stolen or something?" and he grabbed Danny's arm and gave it a little shake.

"I'm trying *not* to tell you anything . . . I mean, I'm not trying to tell you anything . . ." Danny spluttered. "Honest, I only wanted for you to count them. That's all."

"Well, all right." Mr. Teel climbed into his wagon where no one could see him get out the little pouch from wherever he kept it.

"Thirty-seven! Just like I said!" His voice came from the wagon in a moment.

"Including the ones we found today?"

"Of course. They count, don't they?"

Danny tried to groan, as if this was bad news. "Well, any-way, thanks, Mr. Teel. I guess the thregastus is settled now. I'll get back to work."

It was all he could do to keep from singing out for joy. Mr. Teel had *not* lost a diamond. That meant the one Danny had found in the type case came from somewhere else! The chances were all-fired good that Caleb had dis-covered a mine for Danny! But he had better go back to work so nobody would suspect anything. He didn't want anyone to get to his mine before he himself could get there.

"Shucks!" Danny said and broke into a trot toward the *Poor Richard*. Somebody might be robbing him already. If Caleb had put one diamond in the type case, he might have put more. Danny leaped into the wagon and poked eagerly into each of the little square cubbyholes that held the type. The sun had gone down, but it wasn't dark yet, and he could easily see anything odd-shaped or bright among the lead letters with their square smooth sides and backs. One after another, Danny checked off the letters but found nothing until he had almost completed his search. Then—there it was! Another diamond!

"Caleb! You scamp!" Danny breathed. No doubt about it. He held another small, glittering scrap in his hand. "You're killing me, Caleb. Tell me where you got 'em!"

But the crow remained silent and motionless in his place on the wagon bow. He seemed comfortably settled, and nothing Danny did could make him go prospecting again this late in the day.

There was only one thing for Danny now. He had to print the stock, and he proceeded to do just that, carefully going through the process of making each separate impression of the type on the heavy paper Colonel Cluggage had got out for him.

Before long a shout interrupted him, and the twins handed up a sizable dish of beans. The youngsters themselves followed and claimed their reward as soon as he had finished eating.

"What's this for—what's that for?" Their questions were endless, and Danny proudly explained without interrupting the smooth routine of his movements. He hoped to get the job done, or most of it, anyway, before he would need to light candles.

At one point Colonel Cluggage appeared and then disappeared hurriedly with the sheets Danny had finished printing. The stockholders were about to start an official meeting alongside Major Adams' wagon. They would be paying in their money as soon as they could get their stock in exchange. A little while later the bedtime voice of Mrs. Gower filled the air.

"Beatrice! Barnabus!"

Danny waved the twins good night as the last sheets of paper were transformed into imposing-looking stock in the Western Diamond Company.

"What shall I call my mine?" Danny wondered. He wouldn't name it anything small and sleazy like "Western," that was sure. What about "Caleb's Holy Moses Precious Jewel Mining Corporation"?

Danny hadn't finished savoring this when a voice he didn't recognize came to him out of the dusk. "Dan, you alone?"

"Yep. Who's there?"

A figure vaulted into the wagon, and Danny recognized Jack the Jug, the wagoner who had tried to stir up a lynch spirit when he was drunk the other night.

"They're making you work kind of late, aren't they?" the man began.

"I don't mind working when it's exciting like this," Danny answered. He shifted a couple of candles so he could see better. There was only one more sheet to print now.

"I know lots quicker ways to get rich than what you're doing."

Danny gave him a sharp look. Was this fellow by any chance hinting something about Caleb's mine? "Just how's that?"

"Well, for instance, if you were to tell me exactly how to get to that there diamond field of Teel's, I'd make it worth your while."

Danny let out a big breath. The man didn't know Caleb's secret!

"Nope. I promised the major I wouldn't tell a soul. We all had to promise. You'll have to wait till tomorrow and go with the rest of the stockholders."

"Look, young fellow, I'm not waiting till morning. I don't have any money to buy any stock, but I intend to pick up some diamonds before these rich fellows get there."

"Sorry, mister. We promised the major like I said."

"All right!" A new tone had come into the man's thick voice. "You'd better change your mind about telling me. See this?" In the flickering candlelight Danny glimpsed the hunting knife that the man held in his hand. "It won't make any noise between your ribs, and unless you tell me I'll use it on you. They'll think a thieving Indian did it."

Surprise was all that Danny felt at first. He had seen this fellow every day for weeks, when he was sober and in his drunken spells. It had never entered Danny's head that the man had whatever kind of twisted courage it took to carry out a threat of violence all by himself. But a horrified certainty crept over Danny now. This half-crazy drunkard was really ready to plunge the long blade into him if he didn't reveal the location of the diamonds.

Danny stalled for time. "Let me think a minute." Then, grasping for a plan, he added, "Colonel Cluggage will be here any second to pick up the rest of the stock. I'll talk to

you when I'm all finished with my work."

The man seemed to hesitate.

"Now,". Danny thought, "is my chance to throw him completely off balance!" He took a deep breath and bellowed at the top of his voice:

"Colonel Cluggage! Here are some more sheets!"

Terrified, the drunkard jumped down from the wagon and stumbled off into the darkness.

Danny let out his breath and leaned on the press. Now that it was all over, he suddenly felt weak, and his belly muscles contracted as he imagined the knife coming at him.

Vaguely Danny was aware of footsteps approaching, and then the colonel asked somewhat testily, "If you were finished, why didn't you bring the stock over to me?"

"I—I—don't feel well," Danny managed to say.

The colonel looked at him sharply. "You do seem peaked. You'd better roll up in your robe and get some sleep." Without wasting another second, he picked up the remaining sheets of stock and returned to the cluster of men on the other side of the circle of wagons.

"Drat him!" Danny thought to himself. "I've just about

been murdered, and the colonel acts as if I was maybe catching a slight cold."

A second later Danny realized he was expecting the impossible. The colonel had no way of knowing that Jack the Jug had threatened his life. Suddenly Danny stiffened. Jack the Jug was crazy enough to do anything. He might return now that the coast was clear. Quickly Danny blew out the candles, leaped from the wagon, and hurried toward the fire where the stockholders were meeting.

Before he had taken a dozen steps, he heard a terrible scream. It came from the direction of the cavvyard, and it was followed by shrill whinnies and the shaking of the earth that a couple of hundred horses and mules created as they all suddenly tried to gallop with hobbled feet.

"What's that? Utes! Stampede!"

Outlined in the firelight, Danny saw the major standing on the hub of a wagon wheel. "Quiet! Stay inside the circle. Get your guns. But don't a one of you shoot unless I give the order. Flint, you stay here. I'll go see what's happened."

Already the thundering of the animals' hoofs was subsiding, and the major called out above the snorting of the nervous animals, "Who's on guard out there? Are you all right?"

Replies came from a little distance, but Danny couldn't hear what the men said. The stirring and excitement in the wagon circle drowned out the words. It was a while before he shook himself, ran to the *Poor Richard* for his rifle, and crouched in the bed of the almost empty wagon. It was an even longer while before Major Adams returned.

"All right, that wasn't Indians." It was something serious, Danny could tell from the solemn sound of the major's voice. He raced across the circle now, along with most of the other men. "That drunken fool Jack the Jug got himself killed. A horse or a mule kicked him in the head. From the looks of it, he was fixing to saddle up."

"Where in the world did he think he was going this time of night?" someone asked wonderingly.

Only Danny knew the answer.

12

CALEB'S MINE

The next morning seemed to Danny the strangest he had ever spent. First came the burying. Everyone attended except the guards and Colonel Cluggage who said he wanted nothing to do with such a disreputable character as Jack the Jug, alive *or* dead. Major Adams somehow managed to say a few dignified words over the grave of the old reprobate, and thinking about them afterward set Danny to wondering. Jack the Jug had been killed, suddenly, violently, right after he had threatened to murder Danny. Was the man's death some kind of punishment? No! Danny shivered at the thought. That would mean that he himself was in a way connected with it! Nonsense. Jack

175

the Jug died simply because he was too fuddled to handle horses properly. He scared them in the dark, and one of them did exactly what you might expect it to do. To be sure, Jack the Jug had no right to threaten anyone, Danny thought, but he wasn't struck down because he did!

With that load off his mind, Danny watched the second strange event of the morning. A good three fourths of the men in the wagon train eagerly put saddles on horses or mules and hurried up the canyon after Mr. Teel and the major toward the diamond mine in which they now owned shares. The circle of wagons had never before been so deserted.

Half a dozen men, with Flint in charge, remained around camp as guards. One of them stood at the mouth of the canyon. The others fanned out over the sloping sagebrush plain, keeping the cavvyard more or less together.

Before Colonel Cluggage rode off with the others, he told Danny to have the wagon loaded by the time he got back. "Flint and a couple of the guards will give you a hand if you need help stowing the heaviest bundles," he said.

On any other day the prospect of remaining behind

would have given Danny the blues. But this particular morning he was delighted. He would have plenty of time to locate Caleb's Holy Moses Precious Jewel Mine. During breakfast the crow had darted in and out, stealing beans from Danny's plate—a performance that had gone on every morning all the way across the plains. But Danny was studying Caleb with special attention today. For the first time he noticed that the crow didn't eat all the beans he purloined. He hid a few of them. This wasn't really surprising. Caleb was always hiding things. It was *where* he hid them that startled Danny. There was a knothole in the top of the chuck box at the rear of the *Hunkidori*, the wagon belonging to the parents of Bizz and Buzz. Casually, so that he attracted no attention, Caleb landed on the box several times and dropped the beans through the knothole.

Danny couldn't help laughing out loud. Now he knew why the twins were always getting blamed for putting away dirty dishes, in spite of the fact that they stoutly maintained they didn't do any such thing. Caleb was the culprit.

There must be quite a lot of things, Danny suspected,

that he didn't know about his crow.

And how right he was! Almost immediately Caleb
found a new activity on which he could spend his bound-
less energy. He hopped off the Gowers' chuck box, perched
teetering for a moment on the edge of the wagon, then
disappeared under its canvas cover. Danny hurried toward
the *Hunkidori,* planning to lift the canvas and peek. But
his bird reappeared immediately, holding a shapeless object in his beak. With slow, laborious strokes of his wings,
he launched his big black body from the wagon, for all the
world as if he were rowing himself through the air. Moreover, it seemed to Danny that Caleb was dragging an anchor
—something, at any rate, that held him back. Curious,
Danny looked at the wagon from which Caleb had taken
his loot. A gray streak flickered and fluttered over the end
of the *Hunkidori*—gray yarn! And it was unreeling rapidly into space. Caleb had stolen the half-finished sock that
Mrs. Gower was knitting!

Thank goodness the lady herself wasn't in sight. Only
the twins stood near the wagon.

"Buzz! Bizz!" Danny called softly, pointing to the gray

thread. "Look, magic! The yarn is unwinding itself."

"It's bewitched! A wicked sorcerer has put a spell upon it," Bizz said in a dramatic whisper.

"Don't talk that way," Buzz said aloud. "Nothing unwinds itself. Somebody's pulling it."

"It must be somebody who can fly, then. Do you know anybody who's got wings?" Danny asked.

The twins followed the soft gray yarn with their eyes. It went only a little way before it seemed to disappear into thin air.

Buzz pointed to Caleb who was slowly flapping out of sight around the end of a hill. "Yep. *He's* got wings."

"What does Caleb want with Mamma's knitting?" Bizz wondered.

"Probably the same thing he wants with all the stuff he steals," Danny said. "He is trading it for something. He just left you a present in exchange. It's the same present he's been leaving you here-about every day since you started from Independence."

"Why, Danny, don't you say things that aren't so. Caleb hasn't given us any presents!" Bizz exclaimed.

"What do you call this?" Danny opened the chuck box and took out a tin plate on which three moist beans lay. His explanation about them removed a great burden from the twins.

"Wow! Wait till I tell Mamma! She'll have to take back all those scoldings she gave us about putting away dishes that were dirty," Bizz said.

"You and Caleb better watch out," Buzz said to Danny. "She'll scold you instead."

This thought sobered Danny. "Look, when you tell your mother about the beans, just don't say Caleb stole her knitting." He didn't want too many grievances piling up against the crow. Somebody in the wagon train might get exasperated and take a shot at the bird. "If we hurry up, we can find the knitting and she'll never know," he added.

"We're not allowed to go anywhere," Buzz said. "We mustn't go across the stream, ever. Flint said so. Everybody said so."

Of course! Danny realized that the youngsters must not stray away from the wagon train. "I'll be back," he called over his shoulder and trotted off along the gray line of yarn which by now had settled to the ground.

What in the world was that crazy crow thinking of, he thought, flying off in this direction with stolen goods! Any sensible creature would have deposited the knitting near the pot of beans. But wait a minute, maybe Caleb was making some kind of three-cornered deal. Was he trading beans for knitting needles and knitting needles for diamonds? By golly, it was worth looking into, and he would soon find out. He would follow the yarn.

The gray clue led up the hill, but no farther. It stopped abruptly in the top of a scrub oak tree. The knitting needles, still in the half-finished sock, hung there. The yarn had tangled in the branches, jerking the sock and needles from his beak, and so this pirate flight of Caleb's had come to naught.

Caleb himself was nowhere to be seen.

Danny recovered the sock. A little guiltily he broke the yarn, which he couldn't disentangle from the treetop, and began winding it onto a twig as he walked slowly back toward camp. He had quite a ball of it by the time he reached the stream where the twins were waiting for him.

He was about to cross when a screeching "Ah-whooh-wah!"
sounded from behind him.

"Catch!" Danny called, tossing the sock and the ball
of yarn to the twins. "That's Caleb. I have to find him and
give him a talking to."

It wouldn't be a bad idea to give Caleb a scolding, he said
to himself, but some other time. Right now he had better
plans. He hoped the crow would lead him to a diamond
mine. For a second time he started to trot off toward the
hillside where Caleb had disappeared. "Ah-whooh-wah!"
he heard again, louder and closer. From an open spot that
gave him a good view of the country around he saw no
sign of the crow, but a cloud of dust told him that the noise
he had heard was a real stage driver's call, not Caleb's
imitation. The daily coach was a sight he always enjoyed,
and he paused to watch the tall red vehicle sway along the
rough trail, pulled by eight beautiful, galloping horses.

For the last three days armed cavalrymen had accompanied the coaches, riding ahead and behind, an eloquent
announcement that trouble with the Indians was expected.
The Army officers had closed off the mountain portion of

the trail to wagon trains, but the stagecoaches, convoyed by cavalry, went through as usual.

As the cavalcade approached the circled wagons, the driver reined in unexpectedly and stopped. Danny sped back. By the time he reached camp again, Flint and the stage driver had already finished whatever talk had been called for, and the driver's long whip cracked out above the heads of the lead horses.

"What's up?" Danny asked, breathless and disappointed that he had arrived so late.

"Nothing much," Flint answered. "It seems people ahead are worried about why we haven't showed up."

"Did you tell about the diamond mine?"

"Nope. I just gave a kind of vague story."

"Was that all?"

"Well, the driver told me again what we already know. There's a big Ute powwow going on, and we ought to be careful not to stir up Indian trouble. The only new thing he said was that they caught the outlaw that robbed the Mexican rancher in Santa Fe. They even got back all the stuff he stole." Flint sighed. "It just goes to show how much time you can waste being suspicious. Think of all the trouble we'd have been saved if some people around here hadn't suspected that Mr. Teel got his diamonds by stealing them!"

Diamonds, thought Danny! He had set out to follow Caleb to the bird's secret source of supply, and he had got nowhere so far. But with most of the day still ahead, he might locate Caleb in time to keep on his trail to the mine.

Where was that crow anyhow? At a rough guess, Danny could see a hundred square miles of sagebrush from the slope of the hill. Cupping his hands around his mouth, he whistled a signal patiently in every direction. But it brought no result. In the distance a crow did take to the air, and at a dogtrot Danny headed toward it. Before long he knew it was Caleb all right. "Holy Moses! Holy Moses!" the bird screamed as it alternately soared and swooped, soared and swooped.

Danny was puzzled. This was behavior he hadn't witnessed since the wagon train left Independence. Sometimes in the town Caleb had amused himself by teasing dogs that roamed the streets. Squawking, diving, pecking at them and generally bullying, he would drive them someplace where they didn't want to go. But there were no dogs with the wagon train, and surely none in this uninhabited country.

The pursuit continued in a crazy pattern across the landscape. Whatever animal Caleb was chasing, it possessed a desperate will to escape. At last Danny got a good look at the scurrying creature. It was a coyote, as he should have guessed. A coyote looked enough like a dog to satisfy Caleb's desire for something to tease.

Danny sat down under a tree on the hillside to wait. He was at the bird's mercy. He couldn't find Caleb's diamond mine until Caleb was good and ready to go there. Impatiently he watched as the crow-and-coyote race went on. Once it led toward the cavvyard where the guards sat on their horses and kept the grazing animals in a loose herd. Danny held his breath for fear one of the men might take a shot at the coyote and then another, just for the fun of it, at the crow overhead. But the guards were too bored and drowsy in the hot sun to have any interest in target practice.

Danny himself felt drowsy, and without planning it he

dozed off, then fell into a deep sleep.

Two things waked him, a grip on his shoulder and "Holy Moses!" in his ear. Caleb—but it wasn't Caleb. It was Flint McCullough saying, "Holy Moses!"—an angry Flint.

"What kind of business is this? Coming out here to take a siesta and not letting anyone in camp know where you were!"

Danny jumped up, confused at first. "I—I was looking for Caleb."

"The heat has got you," Flint said. "You'd better come on back and start to work. In case you've forgotten, you have a wagon to load."

Danny realized with a hint of panic that Flint didn't know the half of it. Before he could load the *Poor Richard* he had to distribute the type he had set up yesterday. He had to take it apart and put each letter into its own compartment. Swiftly he began the familiar and rather pleasant task, and he grew so occupied that he forgot for the moment his search for Caleb's diamond mine—the search that had ended so ingloriously in a midday siesta. But soon the crow himself appeared and reminded him. The big, glossy black

bird flapped into the wagon and perched on the type case. Deliberately then he leaned over, reached down, picked up a letter that Danny had just dropped in place, then glided to the floor.

Danny chuckled and watched the crow waddling along. Caleb walked underneath the press, paused next to one of the rear legs of the machine, and there dropped the piece of type he held in his beak. Danny squatted on his heels to get a better look at the shadowy place where the thief was hiding his loot. Just under the foot of the press he saw a hole he hadn't noticed before. The board which supported this foot looked as if it had been crushed and broken— probably when the axle broke the day of the big storm. The press, lurching forward as the front end of the wagon sank, must have put too much weight on this corner board and splintered it. The raising of the wagon tilted the machine back into place, and since it was bolted to the floor in several spots it was stable enough to work properly.

But Caleb hadn't finished whatever he was doing in his corner. His beak and part of his head went down into the hole. Then he backed away and strutted out into the open, flapped his big wings, and rose to the top of the type case. He had something in his beak. Danny couldn't be sure what it was, but he made a wild guess. Could it be a diamond?

He didn't stop to wonder how Caleb could get diamonds from under the press; he could only watch with excitement while the crow slowly and deliberately inched along the top of the type case, then leaned forward, poked his head tentatively into one little box and another, and finally opened his beak to let something drop.

Without wasting a split second, Danny jumped toward the case and looked. Among the ink-stained bits of metal, gleamed a small, bright crystal!

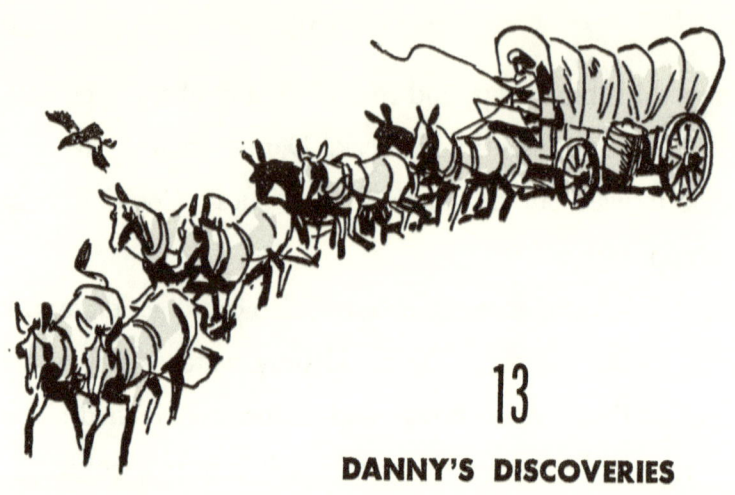

13

DANNY'S DISCOVERIES

Were there more diamonds where this one came from? Danny snatched the little crystal out of the type case, added it to the two he already had in his money pouch, and then on hands and knees crawled under the press.

The hole in the broken board was only large enough for him to get his fingers through. He felt around in every direction. Straight down he touched coarse planks. The wagon had a false bottom!

Danny pondered for a moment. The *Poor Richard* was a Conestoga wagon. Had it been in the smuggler's trade years ago when Santa Fe belonged to Mexico? Was it possible that diamonds smuggled in the false bottom had some-

how been left there and forgotten? Maybe, but what about
Mr. Teel's wagon? His was a Conestoga too, and *it* had a
false bottom and *he* hid diamonds there. Was there some
kind of connection?

Danny's fingers kept probing around in the hole. They
touched a bit of shattered wood and brought it out. It was
not a piece of the floor board of the wagon. This wood was
different—thin, and at one time it had been highly polished.
Fishing around again, he found more splinters. No doubt
about it, a small box had once lain in the hidden compartment, and it had been crushed when the leg of the printing
press rammed through the planking above. On his next try
Danny located a hard, slick little pebble. He caught it
sideways between two fingers and managed to lift it out.
Another diamond! This hole in the wagon floor, this
secret compartment, was Caleb's Holy Moses Precious
Jewel Mine!

"Rats!" Danny said out loud in sheer disgust. The stone
he held in his hand wasn't his to claim, after all the trouble
it had taken. It belonged in the wagon, and the wagon
belonged to Colonel Valentine Cluggage, whether or not

the colonel knew it was there. Danny dropped the diamond back into the hole and stood up, feeling positively grimy with disappointment.

"Hey, Danny! Aren't you ever going to pack this wagon?" Flint called from outside.

"Sure, Flint. I'm packing, all right. But I have to leave a lot of the stuff out till the colonel gets back. The press rammed a hole in the floor, and I have to find out if he wants to fix it before we go on."

"Do you think it's serious?"

"No, probably not," Danny answered. "Don't worry. We'll be ready to roll tomorrow."

If Flint had been in a better mood, Danny might have been tempted to talk the whole diamond business over with him. But the scout sounded edgy.

Hurrying now, Danny stowed into the wagon whatever he could without covering up the broken floor board. He had nearly finished when Flint rode by.

"We've got some visitors," Flint said quietly. "Utes."

Danny jumped down from the wagon, rifle in hand. "Where? What'll we do?"

"The first thing you do is make yourself seem like three or four different people in three or four different places at the same time, and all of 'em as friendly as the dickens. I don't think it's a war party or up to any tricks, but I can't take any chances."

Danny looked puzzled, and Flint explained.

"We don't want the Utes to see how deserted the camp really is. I've put Bizz in the major's wagon and Buzz in Teel's. They are both going to make a racket and talk to themselves. Mrs. Gower will be outside talking to imaginary people in three different wagons. Asa and the guards are going to do likewise."

"Oh, I get it!" Danny said. "I'll be handing stuff up to somebody who is stowing it in the *Poor Richard*." Then a bright idea came to him. "All right if I get Caleb to talk?"

Flint looked a little dubious. "Can you keep him from giving that war whoop of his?"

"I'll try," Danny promised.

"If you don't succeed, I'll wring his neck and yours," Flint said. "That is, if the Utes haven't already done the job for me. Remember, I don't think we'll have trouble unless we give them the idea we're hostile."

"What are you going to do?" Danny asked.

"You watch."

Flint touched his heels to Chiquita and trotted slowly toward a procession the likes of which Danny had heard about but never seen. Four horses and riders approached at a walk along the rutted trail from the direction of Santa Fe. Two men in the lead were riding bareback, and their moccasined feet dangled loosely. In single file behind them came two women, each astride a horse that dragged a big load tied to poles. These drag poles, Danny knew, were the famous travois of the western Indians. On each travois lay a great shapeless bundle wrapped in skins. A small, naked boy sat on top of one bundle, clinging to the rawhide thongs that held it in place. To the other bundle was lashed something that looked like a huge bird cage made of bent willow boughs, and inside it a little, laughing Indian child was playing! The cage was merely a way to keep the baby from falling off!

The men, Danny realized, had no weapons except bows and arrows, and they certainly didn't act dangerous.

In no time, the older Ute sat facing Flint on horseback. Danny watched spellbound as they both began to move their hands in the quick, unbelievably graceful gestures of sign language. Presently Flint dismounted and brought chunks of cloth from the major's wagon. These he handed out to the men, to the women, and then, with a laugh and a flourish, he handed a piece to each of the two children.

The mysterious, silent conversation then resumed, and after a while Flint called across the circle to Danny, "Listen now. These people are going up the canyon. Our party will be coming down. I will ride ahead of our friends the Utes to tell the major they are coming. We don't want anybody to get excited and make a mistake. I won't be gone long."

With that, Flint turned Chiquita into the canyon mouth and disappeared at a gallop. More slowly the Indian party, under its cloud of dust, followed.

Danny went back to loading the *Poor Richard*. The twins, who had been making an uproar in the wagons, climbed down and their noisy play changed in nature.

Danny heard Buzz shouting with glee, "That'll teach

you varmints. . . . I got him." And Bizz yelling, "Hey,
watch out! You almost hit *me!*"

Danny peered around the end of his wagon and called,
"Say, Buzz, who are you varminting over there?"

"Come and see what we've got, Danny," Buzz answered.
"It's a beauty."

When Danny appeared, the little boy proudly displayed
an Indian bow about four feet long. With it he had been
trying to shoot the two arrows Danny had given him, the
arrows Danny had pulled from the side of Mr. Teel's wagon
after the ambush.

"It's pretty hard to make it work right," Buzz said. "You
try it and see."

Danny fitted one of the arrows to the bow and pulled
back. To his surprise, it took real strength to bend the
bow. And when he released the arrow it wobbled crazily
and fell to earth only a short distance away.

"Where'd you get this?" Danny asked. Was it possible
that the Utes who passed by a few moments ago had somehow lost the weapon?

"In Mr. Teel's wagon, of course. You know, that secret

hiding place of his. It was in there," Buzz answered, and then he hurried on to head off possible criticism, "I'm going to put it back, Danny."

This was something new to think about. Why should Teel keep an Indian bow, of all things, in his wagon? What else did he have in that secret compartment? Was it just a coincidence that two wagons in this train had false bottoms with diamonds hidden in them? Would he find another bow in the false bottom of the *Poor Richard?* What did it all mean?

"You put that bow right back," Danny said to Buzz. "Mr. Teel will be here any minute, and he might not like you borrowing it without permission."

While Buzz went off to do as Danny ordered, his sister began to make gestures at Danny, gestures that looked a little like the motions he had seen Flint going through when the scout was talking sign language with the Utes a little while ago.

"Don't you wish you really knew how to talk sign language?" Danny said.

"But I do!" Bizz said. She made a motion with one hand

in front of her face. "That means *friend*. Didn't you see Flint saying that to the Indians? He taught it to me the other day."

"Show me again," Danny said.

Bizz held up her hand, palm forward, in front of her neck, with the first two fingers pointed upward and the others folded down. Then she raised the hand until the tips of the fingers were level with the top of her head. "That's all there is to it. That's what you do when you want to show you're friendly."

"What else do you know?" Danny asked.

But her mind was already on something else. "Look at Caleb! He's stealing stuff again."

"What is it this time?" Danny groaned. "Not another sock!"

"I can't tell. It looked kind of big."

"What did he do with it?"

"He put it in the bean pot."

The pot, Danny discovered, was standing with its lid off on the top of Mrs. Gower's chuck box. Gingerly he reached up to recover whatever his crow had left there, in exchange, no doubt, for some beans. The next moment he stared in complete bewilderment at the thing Caleb had left—a ten-dollar bill.

"Where did that bird go, Bizz?" Danny asked.

"I saw him fly into your wagon."

"Is he still there?"

"I guess so."

Danny hurried to the *Poor Richard* and crawled stealthily along the narrow corridor he had left inside the wagon so that he could show Colonel Cluggage the break in the floor. In the gloom ahead he heard rather than saw Caleb at work in the hole. Presently the bird backed away, straight into Danny's clutches. He let out a squawk of protest, and another ten-dollar bill fluttered to the floor.

"Holy Moses!" Danny exclaimed.

Caleb cheerfully took up the refrain. "Holy Moses! Holy Moses!" the bird chanted and flapped out into the late afternoon sunlight.

Curiosity drove Danny on. He wedged himself under the printing press and felt as far as he could with his fingers into the hole under the wagon floor. But apparently the bird's beak and long neck could probe farther.

Danny hopped out of the wagon and began to rummage in the toolbox attached to its side, looking for something thin enough to use in exploring the secret compartment. A strip of iron, hooked at one end, seemed promising. Back in the wagon, he inserted his tool and worked it around the hole. There was something soft in there all right. Perhaps it was a wad of bills. He pulled it gradually toward him, and as he did so he realized that the hole seemed somehow different from the way it had been before. He could actually see the tool as it waggled back and forth. That was it! He could see! There was some light in the secret compartment, and he was perfectly certain there had been none before. How could that be?

As he worked the soft bundle closer and closer to the hole, Danny kept puzzling about the light. Then he had it! The toolbox, of course; he had left the lid up, and there was some kind of opening from the box into this secret compartment. That was how the light got in!

Concentrating with all his might, he maneuvered the object closer. At last he could get his fingers on it. Money, no question about it. He pulled out a bill, then another. With a fistful of them Danny inched back from under the press. Colonel Cluggage would certainly be amazed when he found out about the treasures hidden in his wagon.

Danny rose to his feet and turned to leave through the corridor he had left among the bundles of cargo. But directly in front of him stood a figure with one arm raised. It was the colonel himself, and on his face Danny saw not amazement but violent anger. In his upraised hand was a revolver held like a club. And that was the last Danny knew.

14

"WHAT DO YOU WANT OF ME?"

"Holy Moses! Holy Moses!"

Somewhere, vaguely, from a place that seemed a long way off, Danny thought he could hear Caleb. The sound came closer—or did it? Where was he? What was going on? The questions tumbled around in a head that throbbed with pain. His arms hurt too. His ankles ached. Danny opened his eyes. Where *was* he?

Around him there seemed to be iron bars. Was he in jail?

Through a fog of panic Danny gradually realized what must have happened. He lay flat on his back, under the printing press, with hands and feet bound to the iron legs of the press, so that he couldn't move a muscle. A gag in his mouth kept him from calling for help.

Above his head Caleb marched back and forth on the canvas wagon cover. The ends of the canvas were closed so tightly that the bird couldn't get in.

Dimly at first, then more clearly, Danny recalled the sight of Colonel Cluggage with arm upraised, an angry, wild look on his face. The colonel must have thought Danny was robbing him of the money hidden in the secret compartment. But why had he tied Danny up?

Thinking was hard because his head hurt so much, but Danny *had* to figure out what was going on. Now, starting over again, the colonel's anger meant that he knew about the secret compartment. This wasn't just an old smuggler's wagon he had bought by chance. The money wasn't there by accident! The diamonds weren't there by accident!

Colonel Cluggage was angry, and he was frightened too! If he hadn't been scared, he wouldn't have knocked Danny out and gagged him and tied him up.

Danny had discovered something that the colonel didn't want anyone else in the wagon train to know!

Panic flowed back over Danny again. If Colonel Clug-

gage was so desperate—so desperate that he had to knock
a fellow out and hide him this way—what else could he do?

Sounds from outside told Danny that the men who had
returned from the diamond mine were eating their evening
meal and arranging to set the guards for the night. Desperately he tried to move a hand or a foot, but each tug
only made the ropes that held him dig painfully into his
flesh. Once he tried to send a signal by banging his already
bruised head on the floor. But the pain was so great he
almost lost consciousness. He knew he couldn't do that
again. Helplessly he asked himself over and over: What
could he do? What could he do?

At one point the sound of Major Adams' deep voice came
from just outside the wagon: "Will you need any help getting the rest of this stuff loaded, Colonel?"

"No, I think Danny will be able to help me in the morning, thanks."

"I must admit, Colonel, I'm surprised at Danny. I didn't
take him for the kind of young fellow that would help himself to anything without asking, let alone a jug of your
whisky. . . ." Major Adams paused.

So that was how Colonel Cluggage had explained Danny's disappearance! He had pretended Danny was in the wagon—drunk! Outrage now mingled with fear, and Danny tried to call out to the major who stood so close. But the gag was tight and the only sound he could utter was a miserable groan.

"The boy sounds in bad shape, all right," the major said. "I hope it will be a lesson to him."

Now it began to come all over Danny what a slick operator this Colonel Cluggage was. He could gag and tie a fellow right in the middle of camp, then tell a story that fooled even the major! What was his game, anyway? Much more important, what did he intend to do to Danny?

Part of the answer came some time later, just at dark, when Colonel Cluggage began to speak in a low voice with another man outside the wagon. At first Danny couldn't be sure who the other person was.

"Now get this through that thick Dutch head of yours," the colonel said. "I don't care how you do it, but you have to bring two horses and tie them to that dead cottonwood a couple of hundred yards up the canyon. Then you'll go back to the cavvyard until the second watch comes and relieves you. I'll be on duty at midnight, and I'll take the station at the mouth of the canyon. You bring the kid there as soon as you come off watch. Have you got it straight?"

"Don't you worry. I know my business. I've done everything else all right. You said yourself the way I fixed that ambush was a work of art. I'll bring the horses all right."

It was Tunis Teel, of course! Danny recognized the voice. Tunis Teel and Colonel Cluggage were partners in some elaborate scheme!

"And don't forget," Teel went on, "it wasn't *my* idea for us both to have the same kind of wagon. That kid was tampering with mine today too. He found the bow I used for the ambush. It wasn't in the right place. He put it back different."

"What about the barrel and ramrod?"

"Those were two things he *couldn't* see. I buried 'em up there beside the gravel pit. I was afraid we might need to do some more planting in a hurry. But I'm worried, anyway. I think the kid saw enough to have us figured out."

"You worry too much!" the colonel snapped.

Danny heard the sound of footsteps moving away. It was probably Teel on his way to start his turn at guarding the horses. What did this all mean? Danny tried to concentrate on the problem. But dizziness from the effort made his headache even worse. Everything went black again. And the next thing he heard was a voice in his ear—Teel's voice.

"All right, kid, wake up. Listen to me. Do just what I say and nothing will happen to you. But if you try anything smart, I'll use this."

Danny felt thin, cold metal against his throat. He could only do as he was ordered. In a minute he stood outside the wagon, on legs that were stiff and painful. His wrists were tied now behind his back. With the knife prodding his ribs, he moved away from the circle of wagons toward the mouth of the canyon.

"It's me!" Teel whispered after a while.

"Come on," the colonel ordered. "I hope you had sense enough not to remove the gag from his mouth."

The new insult provoked only a growl from Teel, and he gave Danny a poke in the ribs that really hurt through his flannel shirt.

Danny shivered from apprehension and from cold too. Night was chilly here at the edge of the foothills. He stumbled on, and the three of them continued up the canyon till they reached the tree where the horses were tied— and where no one in camp could hear, even if he did cry out.

"All right, Teel, take the gag out of Danny's mouth. It must be very uncomfortable," the colonel said, returning to the soft drawl that Danny was used to hearing. "Sorry I had to do this, Danny. Now, make yourself comfortable and we'll talk things over."

This sudden turn left Danny limp with surprise. He had braced himself for a desperate effort to escape from violence, and here was a friendly invitation to relax, although, he noted, the colonel still allowed his hands to remain tied as he perched on a fallen log.

"Danny, I knew you were a capable, ambitious young man when I hired you for this job," the colonel said. "But I confess I didn't know quite how smart you really are. There are nearly forty men in the train, including experienced businessmen, and none of them saw through my little enterprise. You've got a better head on your shoulders than any of them. Do you know what that means? It means I'd value you as a partner, young as you are. Of course, I can't offer you that whole fistful of bills you nearly got away with. Partners share things, you know, and some of the money belongs to Mr. Teel. Some of it, naturally, also belongs to me."

The colonel was wrong, of course. Danny didn't see through his enterprise at all. He only knew that something very strange was going on, and what's more he couldn't understand why the colonel wanted to make him a partner in whatever business he had. Danny needed time to think. Diamonds in false bottoms, a hidden Indian bow, a buried barrel and ramrod—what did they add up to? And why did the colonel think Danny knew the answers? Maybe he would get a clue if he could just keep the men talking. Without really caring what he said, Danny asked, "How about the diamonds and the press and all?"

The colonel, somewhat to his surprise, chuckled appreciatively. "Danny, the more I see of you, the more I respect you. You don't miss a thing, do you? Well, that's the kind of partner I can do business with. All right, you'll get a third of them too."

For a minute Danny acted a part. "You know, Colonel, you interrupted me this afternoon. I didn't have a chance to count the money. How much does it add up to exactly?"

"That's right, you weren't present when the stock was being sold, were you? I got a receipt for exactly twelve thousand two hundred dollars from Major Adams. It will be interesting to see how he handles matters when the stockholders find the cash is missing from his money box."

Danny had to hold back a gasp of amazement. Cluggage had stolen the money that belonged to Teel's mining company! But why was Teel in partnership to steal money from himself?

This was a question that ought to be answered, but it wasn't the most important one right now. Danny couldn't figure out how to behave unless he knew the *real* reason why Cluggage and Teel had brought him out here tonight and offered to make him a partner in a very profitable, crooked deal. Cluggage certainly wasn't the kind of man who would give away a third of more than twelve thousand dollars if he didn't have a very good reason.

"Colonel," said Danny, "you've told me what I'll get if I join up with you, but you haven't said what my contribution is supposed to be. What do you want of me?"

"Frankly, we want loyalty first of all," the colonel answered in a brisk, conversational voice. "That will mean different things at different times, of course. At the moment, I'd like you to tell me honestly just who you've talked to about our little venture and exactly how much you've told them."

Being honest came a lot easier than play-acting, Danny found. The answer to this was simple. "I haven't told a single thing to anybody," he said.

Colonel Cluggage stepped closer to Danny. "You're sure you haven't even given a hint to the major? Or Flint? The Gowers?"

Danny shook his head.

"You must have said something, maybe as a kind of joke, to those youngsters who make such a fuss over you?"

With honesty so obvious that nobody could misinterpret it, Danny replied, "No, sir. I didn't speak to a solitary soul."

Then he went on, "It was only a little while after I found the diamonds in the wagon that I found the money, and I was still finding it when you came."

"Teel!" Colonel Cluggage snapped.

This was not the mild-mannered gentleman who had been speaking a few moments ago. It was someone who was used to giving orders and to having them obeyed no matter what the orders were. This was the man who had dealt Danny a blow earlier today and who could easily do worse than that.

Danny felt bewildered. What had he done to make the colonel's manner change so drastically? His hopes had been rising. By pretending he was willing to work with Cluggage he had thought he could somehow find a way to wiggle out of this mess.

Then, in a sudden flash of understanding, Danny realized what his mistake had been. He had revealed to Cluggage that he alone in all the wagon train had any reason to suspect the colonel was a crook. And Cluggage could now protect himself by one simple act. He could silence Danny forever, or order Teel to do the dirty work for him.

By telling the truth, Danny had signed his own death warrant! Teel, obeying the colonel's sharp command, was edging closer. Danny had to make a break for it, or he would never have another chance.

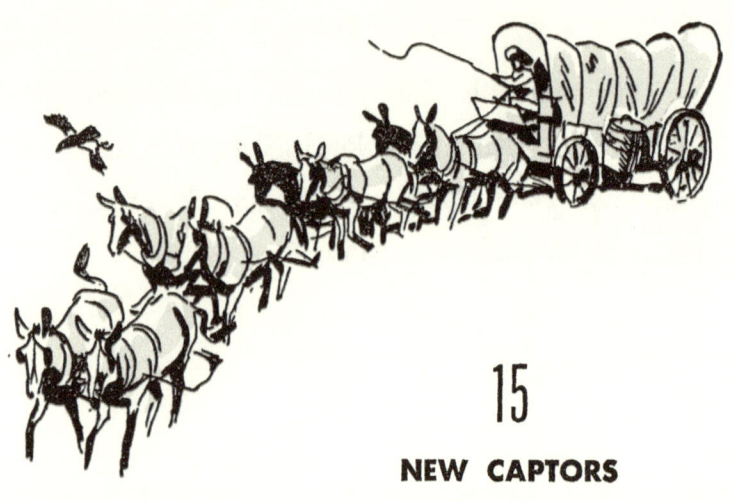

15

NEW CAPTORS

Danny dodged sideways, just as Teel stretched out a hand to grab him. Then he ran. But invisible chains seemed to hold him back, tugging to make him stumble. His wrists were still tied behind his back, and every step was a struggle to keep his balance. To make matters worse, he found he was headed *up* the canyon. He was racing away from the wagon train and possible help!

Too late now! Danny gave everything he had to speeding forward, bent in an awkward posture because of his bound hands. Above his own thundering heart and pounding feet, he heard the quick strides of the two men close behind him. A frenzied surge of energy set his legs to moving

216

faster along the uneven, gravelly trail that led toward the diamond mine. One moment he sped through brilliant moonlight, the next he was in deepest shadow cast by willows and alders that grew along the little stream.

The farther he went, the more surely Danny knew he faced a new danger. His pursuers would shoot as soon as they thought they were far enough from camp so that the sound wouldn't be heard. In the next clump of shadow, he leaped to one side, hoping the men would rush past him and give him a chance to double back toward camp. But Cluggage had thought of that too. His sharp eyes caught the maneuver, and he, too, dodged off the trail. The next Danny knew he had been pulled forward, off balance, down onto the gravel underfoot.

"Teel!" the colonel panted. "I've got him."

Danny lashed out with both feet, fighting to the last moment. But for the second time that day a figure stood above him, arm upraised. Then a revolver struck like a club.

When Danny came back to consciousness, he realized he was lying across the saddle of a horse, face down, tied

there like a sack of meal. Groggily he tried to lift himself
to see what was happening. But the pain was more than his
twice-battered head could endure, hanging down as it was
in an unnatural position. When he opened his eyes again, he
made no sudden move, and slowly began piecing together
the limited information he could gather. The horse that
bore him along was Chiquita, the little sorrel mare Flint
sometimes rode. He could see the scar she had on her right
shoulder. Directly ahead, leading her and riding Tennessee,
was one of the men—Teel. Danny recognized his boots in
the moonlight.

Soon the horses splashed across a stream. They were still
in the bottom of the canyon. How long had he been un-
conscious? Danny had no idea. It was a simple miracle that
he was alive at all. Why hadn't the two men killed him
when they caught him? Danny had absolutely no doubt
that they intended to put him out of the way. Or did Teel
by some chance think he was already dead? Danny tried
to think over all the various hurts in his painful body. Was
one of them a bullet hole or a knife wound? Was he bleed-
ing? As nearly as he could tell he was not.

Then why on earth was Teel taking him anywhere, alive or dead?

Danny turned his head slowly, carefully, and studied Tennessee's rider. Presently the man turned the horse to the right. The moonlight glinted on something in the rifle holster on the saddle. But it wasn't a rifle. It was a strange thing for a man to be carrying in that particular place, and it told Danny an awful story. The metal that reflected the moonlight was going to dig Danny's grave—a shovel.

Now he could see the whole plan. Cluggage and Teel intended to kill him, all right. But they didn't dare do it near camp, where the murder would certainly be discovered. The soil of the canyon bottom was too thin to make a grave possible. They hadn't killed him on the spot when they caught him, simply because they didn't want any bloodstains that would lead searchers easily to his body.

In his tortured position, Danny sensed one more reason why he was being carried some distance up the canyon. If his body was found up here, close to the trail that the Utes followed to their encampment, the Indians would almost certainly be blamed for his murder. Colonel Cluggage, Danny felt sure, was smart enough to think of that. Perhaps he would fix things somehow to look as if Danny had stolen Chiquita and then the Utes had killed him in order to get the beautiful mare.

The misery of breathing, as he jounced up and down on his chest with every step of the horse, the pressure of blood in his swollen, throbbing head—all his pains made him almost wish Teel would hurry and get it over with. But the horses kept on. Teel had turned them into a little side canyon where the soil seemed soft and deep. Here a shovel could take large, easy bites into the earth.

Teel stopped, as Danny had expected he would.

In the methodical way he had, the man dismounted and tied Tennessee to a willow tree, then tossed the shovel to the ground where it landed with ominous metallic clatter. Next he loosened the ropes that held Danny in the saddle and pulled him off onto the ground.

Danny's feet were tied, as well as his hands, and how he would make one final effort at resistance he didn't know. If he could scream and frighten Chiquita, maybe she would kick Teel. But Danny would have to wait for the right

moment. Not now. Teel had stepped out of reach of Chiquita's heels. The man stood, holding her lead rope, as if searching for a good place to tie her.

Suddenly, as he looked at a willow clump, Teel's body went rigid. An involuntary gasp of terror escaped him, and with a speed that amazed Danny he leaped onto Chiquita's back, dug his heels into her sides, and the next moment he was dashing back the way he had come.

A long silence followed, after the sound of the horse's hoofs died away. Danny gathered strength from the quietness, and he struggled to free himself from the ropes. What had got into Teel? What had he seen? He had acted as if he had been bitten by a rattlesnake. Was that possible? No, it was much too chilly for snakes to be active. "Never mind now," Danny thought. If he inched his way around perhaps he would find a solid rock with an edge sharp enough so that he could eventually saw the ropes from his hands. He began worming along awkwardly toward higher ground. There ought to be a protruding rock close to the hillside somewhere.

Danny paused for rest after the first few squirms. This

was slow and painful work. In the silence he was sure he heard something. Maybe it was only the wind in the trees that sounded like men's voices. No, he could swear he heard men talking!

What were they saying? The voices grew nearer, coming from behind him. Could he be seen?

"Help! Come! Help!" Danny called. Then he lurched over on his other side to see if his call was being answered.

There, above him, with dark skin and long black hair glistening in the moonlight, stood two Indian men.

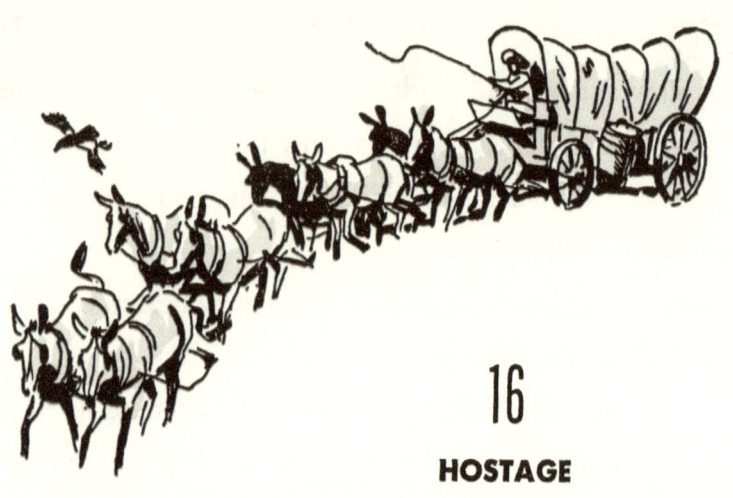

16

HOSTAGE

The voice died out of Danny's throat. He lay staring up in terror and bewilderment. The Indian men stared back at him. But even in his confusion Danny realized they couldn't be any worse than Cluggage and Teel. Tensely he waited for a sign of what they intended to do, and from somewhere he gathered energy for a faint hope that they would let him go free.

"You saved my life. Please untie me," he said at last in as calm a voice as he could manage.

If the men understood, they gave no sign of it. But the older one did speak to his companion. Then the two of them bent over and examined Danny more closely, talked

224

again, and appeared to decide something. The younger man
took out a hunting knife and slashed the cords that bound
Danny's hands and feet.

"Thank you," Danny said with genuine emotion. The
Indians might understand the meaning in his voice even
though they didn't grasp the words. "Thank you."

Painfully then he rolled over and hunched himself up
on his knees. He was surprised to feel a hand on one arm.
The younger man was helping him rise to his feet. Danny
stood irresolute, gingerly rubbing first one wrist then the
other to restore circulation.

Now what? He tried to study the men's faces by such
light as the moon gave. Nothing that he saw made him feel
comfortable and relaxed—no expression of gentleness in
the large, blunt features. If only he knew what they were
thinking! If he could just tell them his grim story! If they
could only talk to each other! The picture of Flint came
to mind, the rapid, graceful hand motions of sign language
he used to establish understanding. Danny wished he had
learned at least a few words of it, the way Bizz had. He
could have learned too, because he and Flint had spent

plenty of time together. Now he was a prisoner of his own ignorance. He couldn't be sure he even remembered the sign for *friend*. Still, it wouldn't hurt to try. The Utes might get the idea that his intentions were peaceful. His arm was stiff from being tied so long, but he managed to raise his right hand in the way Bizz had showed him.

He couldn't be sure in the dim light, but it seemed that a look of animation came to the face of the young man. At any rate, both Indians returned the sign. Then the old one's hands broke into an avalanche of silent oratory.

Sadly Danny shook his head. "I don't understand," he said. "I sure enough wish I did." In a moment or two the Indians seemed resigned to the fact that *friend* was the only word he knew in the inter-tribal, silent language of the Plains.

Again the two conferred. Then, with gestures Danny couldn't mistake, they made it clear that he was to start walking. The young man went with Danny and the other followed, leading Tennessee.

The silver-gray light of daybreak was filling the sky now, and some of it sifted down into the bottom of the little side canyon. Less than fifty yards from the place where Teel had dumped him, Danny came on a small camp. Four hobbled horses grazed near a heap of bundles. Two women rose from the ground and looked with interest and surprise at what the men were bringing home.

"Why, I've seen these people before!" Danny thought. "They came past the wagon train yesterday afternoon." Sure enough, there was the wicker cage on top of a bundle. And here were the two children crawling out from under buffalo robes spread on the ground!

Somehow the sight of a family with children seemed reassuring for a moment. He smiled, or tried to smile. Exhausted and weak, he didn't really know whether he was a prisoner or a guest, but he did his best to look calm and unworried.

"Hello!" he said and fished into his pocket. There were two pennies in his pouch, and he offered them. One of the children took the penny unabashed. The other hid his face shyly behind his right hand while the left reached out for the gift.

The women looked on gravely. In a moment one of them

turned away, then came back holding out a rawhide container. Danny couldn't understand her gesture. To show her meaning she reached into the container, took something out, and put it in her mouth.

Food! Suddenly Danny felt famished. "Thank you," he said and helped himself to something that seemed to be dried meat. It was tough and strong-tasting. Slowly he ate one mouthful, then another.

Meantime, as the light grew more clear, the Indian women packed their travois, including in the bundle, Danny noticed, Teel's shovel. Then they put the smaller child in his cage and the other on top of the bundle where he had been riding yesterday.

As Danny chewed on the tough jerked meat, he wondered if by some miracle the men were going to turn him loose. Or were they just giving him a polite last meal before they killed him and took possession of his horse? The questions answered themselves in a way: For the present, the Indians weren't going to do anything. They made it clear that Danny was to go with them, but on foot. He had to walk between the two mounted men, while the younger one led the colonel's horse, Tennessee.

It was a neat arrangement. Without tying him, without threatening, they had him completely at their mercy. The men carried bows and arrows, hatchets and knives; Danny had only his bare hands. He couldn't possibly escape. He was as much a prisoner as he had been last night when his hands and feet were tied. But at least he was alive, and he wouldn't have been if Teel hadn't been scared by the Indians. He would be lying in a grave, dug with the shovel that now jounced along on the travois.

Digging seemed to be Teel's specialty, Danny thought with a grim smile. First diamonds, then a grave—in one case, taking something out of the ground, in the other putting something back.

The sun played full on Danny now as he walked along between the two horses. The pace was slow and comfortable enough. Nothing was going to happen to him, at least until his captors delivered him to the big Ute powwow which Danny assumed was their destination. At last he had a chance to think through all the puzzling things that had been happening.

First of all, Cluggage and Teel weren't strangers to each other. What a pair of actors! They had been in cahoots for a long time. Whatever they were up to, they had planned it out months ahead, and their meeting here at the mouth of the canyon had been carefully scheduled! That was quite a trick too, although of course the daily stagecoaches did carry mail back and forth.

Did their scheme, whatever it was, concern diamonds? Both of them had diamonds in the false bottoms of the wagons. Had Teel turned over a mess of them to Cluggage in the last few days? No, he couldn't have. Danny felt absolutely certain that the colonel's diamonds had been in his wagon all the way across the Plains, hidden in the litttle box that was crushed when one leg of the press broke through the false floor. The colonel must have been bringing diamonds *to* the diamond mine!

The meaning of this almost took Danny's breath away. Cluggage and Teel were somehow faking the mine! Major Adams had said diamonds didn't exist in the Rocky Mountains, and he was right.

But how could that be? Danny had picked up with his

own fingers a diamond that had been dug up in front of his very eyes. Nobody could have planted it there, either. It had come from a spot, chosen by the major, where Danny was sure the gravel couldn't have been disturbed. Nobody could have planted it there.

Planted? Wait a minute! He had heard the crooks use that very word when they had him tied up inside the *Poor Richard!* What did they say exactly? Something about a barrel and a ramrod—that must be a gun barrel. Did they plant diamonds by shooting them into the earth?

No, that didn't seem likely. How could a little crystal be shot through almost a foot of gravel? Was there any other way to get a diamond under a foot of gravel without digging a hole, putting it in place, and piling the gravel back? Barrel and ramrod—barrel and ramrod—suddenly Danny knew! You could put the ramrod into the barrel, then force the two of them down into the gravel, withdraw the ramrod, drop a diamond down the gun barrel. Then you would withdraw the gun barrel. There would be no signs of digging, because you wouldn't have *been* digging.

What about the money, then? How did Cluggage get

it out of the major's strongbox? And when did he steal it? These were questions that had no quick answers, and they would have to wait.

Danny's party emerged from the woods through which their trail had been winding into a rich mountain meadow. Here, he knew, was the place where his fate would be settled. Here stood the big encampment. In this spot the question of war or peace with the Indians might be determined.

At least a hundred tepees, set in irregular rows, made up the camp. In front of each one of them stood the grim reminder that the Utes were a nation of warriors. Saddles lay on the ground, ready to be flung onto war ponies. Shields leaned against the tepee entrances. And stuck in the ground, ready to be grabbed, were spears—some with stone points, some tipped with pieces of iron filed to razor sharpness. The scores of dogs even seemed to have an aggressive air. They snarled and snapped at each other and at Danny's party.

Small boys, who had been practicing marksmanship with bow and arrow, dropped their martial game long enough to run and stare at the white prisoner whom the newcomers were bringing in.

Danny's arrival sent a wave of excitement through the whole camp. Women and old men came from tepees. It seemed to Danny that a thousand pairs of black eyes bored into him, and a thousand tongues asked, "What is this outsider doing here? Why did anybody bother to bring the intruder in alive?"

Hoping it would do some good, Danny made the sign for *friend*. He made it over and over again. But not a hand went up to return his greeting. He felt sure the Indians knew what he meant; they simply chose not to be friendly.

At last, in desperation, he called out, "Anybody here speak English?"

So many people had gathered now that his little party was completely surrounded and could not move in any direction. "Anybody speak English?" he called again.

Surely someone among all these hundreds knew at least a few words.

Finally a man whose braids were streaked with gray stepped forward. "I speak," he said.

"I am not an enemy," Danny explained hastily. "Please tell these people to let me go back to the wagon train."

"We kill spies. We don't send them back to tell how many warriors we have," the elderly man answered.

"But I'm not a spy! I didn't want to come here!" Danny protested. "Ask those men how they found me."

The interpreter spoke to Danny's captors. Then he motioned for Danny to follow him. A way for them opened through the silent, unfriendly crowd. Where were they going? Was he on his way to be executed as a spy? Danny could see no possibility of escape. A thousand hands were ready to grab him if he tried to run. Hoping he didn't show the fear he felt, he stepped from this visible danger into a tepee where unknown dangers might be waiting.

Though the light was dim here, he easily made out two figures—two unforgettable figures—the twin chiefs, Kanneatche and Curicata, sitting crosslegged on a buffalo robe beside a small fire. Kanneatche, big and fat, still wore his stovepipe hat. Thin, wispy Curicata had a mirror propped up in front of him, and he was painting a red, blue, and yellow design on his face.

In the tense minutes that followed, Curicata continued looking at himself, perfecting the design which Danny fearfully guessed was war paint.

After a few words from the interpreter, the elder of Danny's captors spoke. Kanneatche plainly asked some questions, then addressed one to Danny, which the interpreter translated: "What are you doing here?"

Danny explained, amid frequent aggressive interruptions from the chief. "I didn't want to come here," Danny finished. "This man forced me to come. Please give me my horse and let me leave."

Nothing in Kanneatche's belligerent appearance suggested sympathy for Danny's plight. "When I was your age," he said, "white men came from the direction of the rising sun. They promised they would only pass through our lands. They said they would not bother us. Since then every year when the grass gets green, more and more and more white men come. Always they make promises, and always they lie. The chief of your wagon train promised he would not stop. But he did stop."

"But I explained that," Danny protested.

"There are always explanations for every promise made to my people and then broken. More and more white men come. And when they come they kill our buffalo and scare away the deer. They leave us no food, and they want to live on our land. Now you tell me a story about bad men in your wagon train. You want to keep bad men from hurting good men, you say. Why should we care about that? We think all white men are bad. They all try to steal our land. The more time they spend hurting each other, the less time they will have to hurt us."

Danny was shocked and surprised. The next moment he felt utterly hopeless. If this was the way the Utes thought, he would never get away alive. Still he had to keep trying.

"I've never done anything to hurt you," he said. "How can you be angry with me?" Then he had another thought. "If you really want that wagon train to leave, the best thing you can do is let me go free. Major Adams will send men to look for me. If your men and his men start shooting, the soldiers will come. You'll have much more trouble if you keep me than if you let me go."

For the first time Curicata spoke. "Why should we believe that Major Adams will try to find you? How do we know that your people were not trying to leave you behind when they tied you up and brought you to the place where our people found you last night?" With a glint in his eyes he added, "How do we know your people won't be very angry if we send you back?"

Again Danny was caught off balance. While he was trying to think how he could reply, a young man clad only in breechclout and moccasins stepped into the tepee and spoke to the seated chiefs. What he had to say seemed to interest them greatly. The interpreter said to Danny, "This scout tells us that your wagons have not left. Many men carrying guns are riding in every direction out of your camp. Chief Kanneatche wants you to tell him what this means."

"I am sure it means they are looking for me and my horse."

Kanneatche listened to the answer to his question. Then he said, "Your Major Adams has found another excuse for staying here. But he will be sorry. We have decided to attack your people if they have not left by dawn tomorrow."

The immense importance of this announcement silenced Danny. Just because of him, the entire wagon train might be wiped out. An Indian war would start. What could he do? *What could he do?* Then, all of a sudden, he saw the whole thing clearly. If he could only make the chiefs see it too!

"Do you want the wagon train to leave? Then you will have to let me go. Do you want white men to stop riding up the canyon and digging in the earth there? You will have to let me go. If you keep me here, the wagon train will stay and there will be fighting. If fighting starts, soldiers will come and do more fighting. You will kill many white men, and many of your warriors will die too. But when fighting is over, *more and more white men will come riding up the canyon to dig there.* They think there are little stones of great value in the earth in the canyon. The men who tried to kill me told them that the stones are there. These men tried to kill me because I discovered they were telling a lie. *There are no valuable stones in the canyon.* But I am the only one who knows this. I am the only one who can prove to my people that they will never find any valuable stones in the canyon. That is why you must let me go."

Curicata listened to the translation of this, and without looking up from his mirror, he said, "The white boy is clever. He thinks of good arguments to save his life. But how can we know that he will make his people move on? Perhaps he will only warn them to prepare a trap for us when we attack tomorrow morning."

"You don't know! You can't know!" Danny shouted in exasperation. "But there will be a war if you keep me. Anybody can see that!"

Before either of the twin chiefs got around to saying anything that they wanted the interpreter to translate, Danny heard sounds of a galloping horse, and another young man in breechclout and moccasins entered the tepee.

The chiefs listened to him, then the interpreter again told Danny to explain the meaning of what the scout had seen. Clearly, this second scout had no knowledge of what the first one had reported, because he had been stationed near the trail farther north. He, too, had seen armed men from the wagon train, and he described two of them in

detail—Cluggage and Teel! And they were riding toward
Raton Pass at top speed.

Now a brilliant idea came to Danny. It was risky, but
it answered Curicata's doubts; it gave the Indians a guarantee that Danny was not trying to play some kind of
trick.

"I'll tell you what your scout's report means," Danny
said, full of excitement. "The two men riding north are
the bad men who tried to kill me. They are the bad men
who tried to cheat the others in the wagon train. They are
pretending to look for me, but they will not come back
to the wagon train. They are trying to escape. Now, I will
change the request I made of you a little while ago, and
I will offer you proof that I am not lying. Give me my horse;
tell several young men with very fast horses to come with
me. Tell them to lead me by the shortest trail to the pass.
Tell them to help me capture the two bad men. Then you
can keep me a prisoner—a hostage—until the wagon train
leaves. All I ask is that you send a message to Major Adams.
Tell him exactly what has happened. He will believe you,
because he has told me you are men who keep your word.

But we must go at once. I cannot go alone, because I do not know the way."

The twin chiefs were silent. Danny's fate and the fate of the wagon train depended on what they decided.

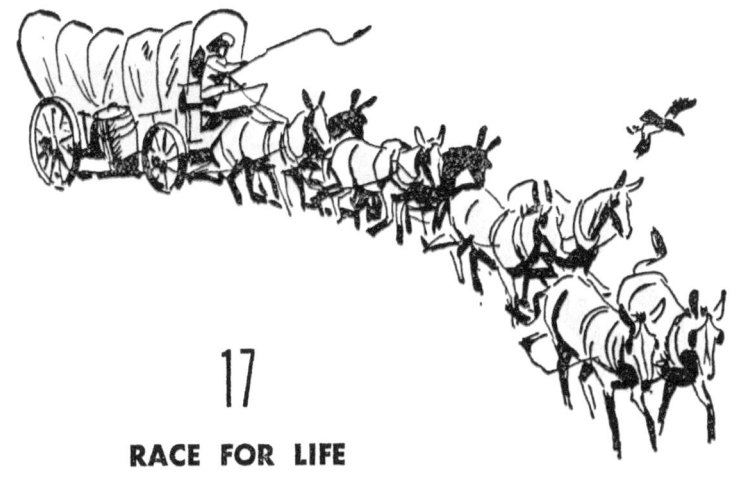

17

RACE FOR LIFE

"I did it!" Danny told himself joyfully as Tennessee broke into a gallop. "I convinced 'em!"

He had, indeed, swayed the twin chiefs by the arguments he had used in that strange, early-morning council. And once the Utes had made their decision, things began to happen with amazing speed. In no time, four well-armed warriors, stripped down to their breechclouts, had mounted their best horses. Two of them brought lariats along, which had been Danny's idea, and two of them spoke English— which was a blessing.

The goal of the little party would be Raton Pass, where they hoped to arrive in time to lay a trap for the fugitives,

243

Cluggage and Teel. Chief Kanneatche had assured Danny that the Indian path through the high country was quicker than the wagon road up the canyon bottom. If Danny and the warriors rode hard, they had a good chance to make their mission a success.

The Indian ponies were fresh. Would Tennessee be able to keep up with them? The horse had worked yesterday, again last night. Danny, leaning forward in the saddle, stroked the animal's sleek neck and felt muscles that were alive with excitement. Tennessee seemed to think he was in competition with the ponies, and there was nothing he loved better than a race.

Sooner than Danny expected, the mountain path afforded a view of the broken prairie country far below. There lay the Santa Fe Trail, a dim line of wagon tracks through the sagebrush. The first quick glance revealed no sign of horsemen. Danny looked again—and again. At last, almost at the mouth of the canyon that led up to Raton Pass, he glimpsed a telltale streak of dust in the air. Cluggage and Teel were far ahead. Danny groaned. How could he and the Utes possibly overtake the two fugitives?

But if the Utes were discouraged by the sight, they didn't show it. They leaned low over their horses' necks and kept their quirts busy.

Now the path turned to avoid a deep gully, and when Danny next saw the dust cloud below, it had moved on into the canyon. The road there, he knew, was steep, and it would get steeper. Cluggage and Teel would have to let their horses climb slowly. The mountain path, on the other hand, turned out to be almost level, which meant that Danny and his four companions could maintain their steady, swift pace.

The path and the wagon road drew steadily closer together. When Danny looked down now, he could see clearly defined horsemen, not mere specks in front of a cloud of dust. Ahead lay the meadow that stretched across Raton Pass itself. The path and the road entered the meadow at almost the same point, and step by galloping step it grew clearer that Danny would beat his opponents to the goal.

"Stop!" Danny called out to the Utes. "Stop here!"

In a moment the five horses stood in a restless circle.

"This is what you must do," Danny began, and the four warriors looked at him sharply. Their prisoner—a white boy at that—was giving them orders. "First we will ride along the edge of the meadow to the wagon road. Then we will follow the road down into the canyon a little way to that clump of willows. You two"—he indicated the Utes who had not brought lariats— "must stay behind the trees. When you hear me shout, you must fire your guns into the air." Then, turning to the other two men, he went on, "Leave your horses at the willow trees. Bring your rifles and your lariats. I will leave my horse and go with you. Then I'll show you what to do next. Let's go!"

Amazingly, Danny realized, he was in full charge and the Utes were ready to obey him. All five horses streamed along the edge of the meadow toward the clump of willows.

Danny flung himself off Tennessee and said to the two who had lariats, "We'll hide ourselves behind those big rocks ahead. When the white men ride past, I will talk to them. I'll try to persuade them to drop their weapons and surrender."

For the first time the Indians looked suspicious and

puzzled. "Why should you let them know that we are here?" one warrior asked. "Why don't we just shoot?"

"We must capture the men alive!" Danny said with deep urgency in his voice. "Your chiefs agreed to this. I have no time to explain. You must catch them with your lariats."

"What if we throw our ropes and miss?" the Ute asked.

"Shoot their horses—" Danny began, then stopped when he saw the dismay on the faces of these horse lovers. "Well, then, make the horses buck them off and if the men start to run, shoot at their feet. But don't kill them. Come now. Hurry!"

"Here, take this," said one of the warriors who was remaining at the willow clump. He handed Danny a revolver.

For a split second Danny hesitated. The Utes had made it clear they would go along on his harebrained expedition on condition that he carried no arms. That was easy to agree to, because he had no arms to carry. But what did the warrior mean now, thrusting the weapon on him? Was this a trick?

Impatiently the man waggled the revolver. "Take it. You may need it!"

Danny hesitated no further. "Thanks," he called back over his shoulder as he ran. The warrior's gesture was a solid expression of confidence. It gave Danny a good feeling as the big moment approached.

Together with the Utes he sped down the wagon road toward a series of large boulders that bordered the wheel tracks.

"You hide here," Danny panted. "I'll hide on top of this rock. When the white men come, I will talk to them. I'll tell them to drop their weapons. Then when I whistle, you will throw your lariats. You rope the first man. Tell your friend to catch the second one."

Instantly the two warriors leaped behind the tall rocks that would hide them from anyone coming up the wagon road. Then they opened the loops in their lariats and stood poised, ready to make their throws.

Danny scrambled to the top of his rock and stretched out so that none of him was exposed to view. Preparations for the ambush were complete.

Tensely Danny listened. The slowly approaching rattle of hoofs against stone told him that Cluggage and Teel suspected nothing. They were walking their weary horses steadily up the trail. Soon he could hear the deep panting of the animals.

As the moment came near, he wanted to shout out with fierce joy. He was about to trap the two men who had held him prisoner only a few hours ago, a prisoner bound and gagged and headed for his grave. Restraining himself, he clung close to the rock, while the horses plodded nearer. Cautiously he raised his head at last. Cluggage rode in front. He passed the rock where one Ute was hiding. Four steps, three steps, two—he was just where Danny wanted him. And Teel? He was in position too. Now!

"Stop where you are!" Danny shouted. "Drop your guns!" His voice sounded so loud that it seemed to be the only thing in the canyon. "Colonel Cluggage! Mr. Teel! Drop your guns! You're surrounded!"

The men stopped, looking thoroughly startled. But they did not drop their weapons. Instead, they peered eagerly among the jumble of huge rocks to see where Danny was hiding. The Utes, meantime, had got themselves back out of sight.

"Danny!" the colonel called, assuming his pleasantest tone. "You had me worried. Where have you been? I was afraid the Utes might have got you, and I wouldn't have wished that on you for the world. You can come out now. We won't hurt you."

"*You* won't hurt *me!*" Danny spluttered. This man Cluggage certainly had his nerve. "I said *drop your guns*. You're surrounded by Ute warriors. They would rather kill you than take you alive. And they'll shoot you if you don't do as I say. It's no use trying to run for it. There are Utes ahead of you. There are Utes right here and behind you." He wished now he had thought to post one of the warriors below, but if Cluggage and Teel believed him, that was all that counted.

The colonel, however, kept up his show of self-assurance. "Danny," he said, talking up to the blank rock above him, "don't you think it's about time to quit playing games? I know you're up there. Come on down where we can have a serious, friendly talk."

"All right, fire!" Danny yelled at the top of his voice. "Fire away!"

Two shots roared out from behind the willow trees.

"Now do you believe me? Throw down your guns!"

Teel, white where his beard didn't cover his face, searched with frantic eyes for a hiding place somewhere—anywhere.

"Drop your gun before it's too late, Teel!" Danny shouted.

The man let his repeating rifle fall with a clatter to the ground.

"Fool!" Cluggage snarled at him, then dug his heels suddenly into his horse. "Giddap! Git!"

At the same instant, Danny whistled his signal to the Utes with the lariats. The colonel's horse reared, surprised by the blasting whistle and by his rider's sudden kick. And as he reared, a Ute lariat sailed out over the spot where the colonel had been. A good throw, but a miss!

"Wait!" Danny stood up and shouted to the disappointed lariat thrower. "Don't shoot!"

The other roper found his mark. His loop fell around Teel, tightened on his arms, and pulled him off his horse before he knew what had happened. Instantly the roper stood over him, knife in hand.

For crucial moments, the colonel struggled to regain control of his horse. Then he saw the Ute standing over Teel, and he reached for his revolver. But quick as he was, Danny was quicker. He leaped from his vantage point on the rock and crashed down into Cluggage. Crack! went the revolver, but the bullet missed its goal, and Danny's catapulting weight carried the man to the ground. For a moment the slender Cluggage tried to free himself from Danny's grip. Then he saw a Ute standing over him, rifle in hand, and he gave up. "I guess you've got me," he said.

The Indians' stiff horsehair lariats were not very handy for tying the prisoners, Danny discovered. He could see why the Utes preferred the long strips of rawhide with which they soon had Cluggage and Teel trussed up and helpless on the ground.

While the four Indians looked on with interest, Danny opened the colonel's saddlebags and saw what he was absolutely sure he would find: quantities of five-, ten-, and twenty-dollar bills, together with a pouch of gold pieces and another which he could tell by the feel held diamonds.

"These belong to my friends in the wagon train," Danny said to the Indians, and he transferred to Tennessee the saddlebags from the horse the colonel had been riding.

On the spur of the moment, Danny decided that Cluggage and Teel owed something to the Utes for all the trouble they had caused.

"Colonel," he said, "I expect you know that you made Major Adams break the promise he made to the twin chiefs that he'd not stop on their lands. You nearly stirred up a Ute attack on the wagon train. And in case you don't know it, I can tell you that you almost set off a full-scale Indian war. Wouldn't you like to show you're sorry? For instance, you could give me Tennessee to make up for the trouble you've caused me. And you could give these men the horses that you've been riding this morning."

The colonel let out a sound halfway between a growl and a bellow.

Danny turned to the Utes. With a broad grin he said, "This white man speaks a queer language. I will translate. He says he gives you these two horses—and their saddles."

The Utes exploded with laughter at Danny's joke.

"And here," Danny went on, tossing the revolver back to its owner. "Thanks for trusting me." Then he paused. He hadn't planned any farther ahead than this. "I suppose," he said at last, "we should turn these men over to the soldiers when they come riding with the next stagecoach. And as for me, I am still your prisoner. What do you want to do with me?"

The look of amazement and confusion on the face of the colonel was almost reward enough by itself for all that Danny had been through.

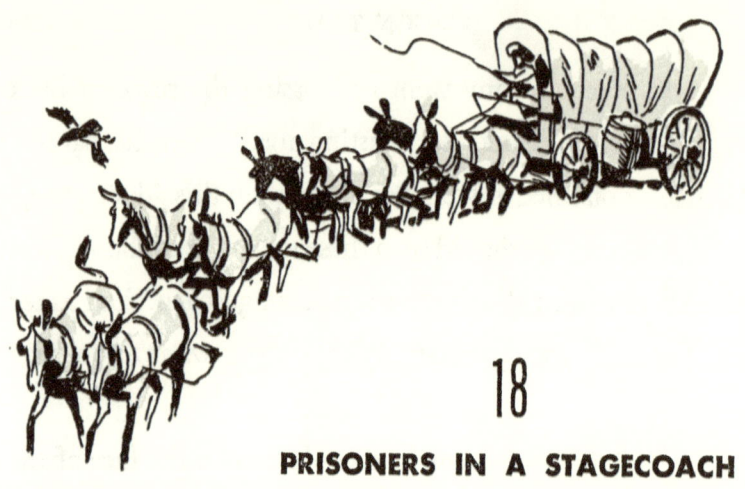

18

PRISONERS IN A STAGECOACH

Danny suddenly realized that maybe he had been a little bit too theatrical when he insisted on reminding the Utes that he was their prisoner. The warriors stood to one side and began talking earnestly in low voices, and Danny was the subject of the conversation.

At last one of the men came forward. "We go to our camp now. We have good new horses and saddles. We have good new guns."

For the first time Danny noticed that the Utes hadn't waited for him to give them the weapons that belonged to Cluggage and Teel!

"These are good," the warrior went on. "You are good,

you are nice boy. We don't want you."

Danny grinned. He couldn't remember when he had been so pleased by inconsistency, and by not being wanted. "Weapons are good, so you take them. I'm good, so you leave me!" he chuckled.

The warrior smiled back.

"Before you go," Danny said seriously, "I want you to give me your word you won't let any of your men attack Major Adams' wagon train today. You have my word that the wagon train will leave early tomorrow morning. You know now what the whole story is."

"No war today," the Ute said with a cheerful grin. "No war today."

With that, two of the warriors climbed aboard their newly acquired horses. The stirrups hung down much too long for them—the Utes were short people—and Danny wondered for a moment why they made no attempt to adjust the stirrups. Were they so used to riding bareback that it wasn't worth the trouble? Or were they proud men who wanted to conceal the fact that they didn't know how to handle the white men's saddles? Well, he would never know the answer. The party moved off and were soon driving the extra animals ahead of them along the mountain path that led back to their encampment. And Danny was very much alone, without a weapon, in charge of two men who only hours ago had tried to murder him. Nothing kept them from making a second attempt, he felt sure, but a few strands of rawhide around their wrists and ankles. Almost automatically he picked up the broken limb of a tree from beside the road. Here in this club was a kind of protection at least.

Now the full size of his problem began to dawn on Danny. He wanted first of all to know how long he was going to have to wait here. It was possible that today's westbound stagecoach had already gone down the canyon, early this morning before he had begun to observe the road. Although the coaches left Independence daily on schedule, many things could cause delays in the six hundred miles between here and there. You couldn't tell what time of day or night a westbound coach might come over the pass. By and large, the eastbound coach, which was still close to its starting point, put in its appearance toward midafternoon. Danny hoped he wouldn't have to wait that long before seeing another human being and having a chance for a bite to eat and water to drink. The sun was almost directly overhead now, and it beat down intensely on the three of them in the middle of the road.

Danny glanced at his prisoners. They looked uncomfortable, but there was nothing he intended to do about it. He was sure that if he tried to drag either of them into the little shade of the tall rocks, Cluggage would find some way to trick him, and before he knew it he would be at the colonel's mercy again. But it would do no harm to ask a question.

"Has the stage from the east come by yet today?"

At one and the same moment Teel said, "No," and Cluggage said, "Yes!"

"You just proved to me that it has *not* come yet," Danny said, enjoying himself thoroughly.

"Of course it hasn't come," Teel growled.

"Young man, you interest me," Cluggage remarked in that pleasant, refined drawl of his. "What leads you to your conclusion?"

"Well, you thought I might be discouraged if I saw a very long wait ahead, and if I was discouraged your chances of escape improved," Danny replied.

But the colonel was too uncomfortable to maintain his interest in a conversation as he lay sweating in the dust of the rutted road. Danny himself felt uncomfortable. There was nothing to do but wait—how long he couldn't guess— and certainly he was going to wait in the shade. Or was he? He looked around and could see no place this side of the willow trees which would provide both shelter from the sun and a full view of his prisoners. Somehow he just wouldn't feel safe if he went off as far as the willows. With a sigh he leaned back against a rock. He remembered what had happened to him yesterday when he sat down to rest. He was twice as tired now, for he had been hit on the head, tied up, had gone without sleep most of the night, and then had galloped for miles to ambush these two.

He was terribly tired and terribly thirsty. Whatever stream fed the willows here had dried up in the August heat. His only hope for water was a thundershower. A glance skyward showed him huge clouds which would deliver a shower someplace today, but whether on him he could not guess. Every aching inch of him yearned for water, food, and sleep. Two of these prized items he couldn't get, and the third he dared not take. He closed his eyes for a second and nearly dozed off standing up. No matter how difficult it was going to be, he had to force himself to walk to keep himself awake. Slowly he began to do sentry duty near his captives.

Perhaps half an hour passed, and then he was certain a faint rumble came from the meadow at the top of the pass, a rumble and then a vibration of the earth that announced the pounding of horses' hoofs! The stage! It must be! Danny trotted up the road. He had to make sure the stage stopped before it ran over Cluggage and Teel.

"What's the trouble?" a cavalryman demanded as he reined in his mount.

"I've got two outlaws—" Danny began.

But before he could finish, Cluggage called out in the brisk, convincing voice he could assume, "Arrest that boy. He's a thief. You'll find thousands of dollars he's stolen in the saddlebags on his horse."

"What's going on here?" the cavalryman shouted, as the stagecoach rattled to a halt behind him. Then he turned to the five other riders in the convoy. "Keep me covered. I'm going to investigate. This has the earmarks of some kind of trap."

"Look here," Danny said earnestly, "those men stole the money and they're trying to blame me."

The cavalryman stared at him, and Danny realized that his words didn't make much sense if you didn't know what had happened. Besides, he certainly must not look very impressive. He hadn't washed since yesterday. Dried blood matted his hair where the revolver handle had cut his scalp, and his clothes were even dirtier, if possible, than he was.

The colonel, however, managed to look like a colonel, tied up though he was and lying in the dust. "Release me!" he ordered. "Where's the officer who's in charge of this detail?"

"Hey, Sergeant!" the cavalryman shouted. "Here's something that's in your department!"

A mustachioed young man with sergeant's stripes

cantered up. "What in the world have you got here?" he asked.

"You tell me!" the private answered. "I'm plumb buffaloed."

In an icy, commanding voice, Cluggage said, "If you will be kind enough to release me and my friend, I'll give you an account of that wayward youth's actions. I'd advise you to keep an eye on him. Take care he doesn't escape. He's slippery."

"Sergeant, I demand the arrest of these two men for robbery and all kinds of monkey business," Danny said desperately.

"Nobody's going to escape," the sergeant said with a swagger. "Can't be any harm in letting these two men stand up. Pritchard, cut 'em loose."

The private whipped out a knife and slashed the rawhide thongs. "Don't often see this kind of thing," he said to the sergeant. "The kid seems to know how to use rawhide Indian-fashion."

"I didn't tie 'em up," Danny said. "The Utes did."

The sergeant drawled, "Are you sure you haven't been

out here in the sun too long?"

Cluggage, with a kind of graceful ease, brushed the dust out of his clothes and said to the sergeant, "Let me tell you the whole story. We are all from Major Seth Adams' wagon train. It is stopped several miles ahead of you. Yesterday most of the men in the train were out of camp. This boy here, whom I foolishly employed to drive my wagon, was left in camp. I returned and found him intoxicated—on liquor of mine that he had stolen. Sometime last night he robbed Major Adams' strongbox, taking more than twelve thousand dollars. He stole my best horse and my saddle and headed east. This gentleman, Mr. Teel, and I overtook him right here. But the boy played some tricks and we had bad luck. He turned the tables on us and captured us. He was just about to leave us here to be run over by the stage when you appeared. You came so suddenly he didn't have time to get on his horse. So, of course, he cleverly stopped you and accused us of the crime that actually he committed."

"Well, sir, that's quite a situation," the young officer said. "Quite a situation."

"Yep, it do beat all," Teel chimed in. "Every single man in the wagon train is out hunting for the kid because he stole their money. You'll find that out when we get back."

The sergeant asked then, "What's this the young fellow said about Utes?"

"Who knows why he thought that whopper up!" Cluggage said.

"Yep, he can lie faster than you can ever listen," said Teel.

The way these two worked was so fascinating, Danny forgot for a minute the trouble he was in. Actually it would be very difficult to demolish the colonel's convincing story!

"Sergeant," said the colonel with finality, "I don't want to hold you up any longer than necessary. You take the saddlebags—they're on the horse the boy stole from me. They've got the money in them. You take charge of the money and I think Mr. Teel would appreciate it if the coach gave him a ride back to the wagon train. I'll stay here long enough to round up the two horses, the ones Mr. Teel and I were riding. This young scoundrel chased them off up the mountainside somewhere."

With his customary quick, efficient motions, the colonel started toward Tennessee.

Suddenly it dawned on Teel what the colonel was up to. Cluggage meant to salvage the diamonds from the saddle-bags, mount Tennessee, and escape over the pass, leaving Teel to his fate.

"No, you don't!" the big man bellowed. "Those horses are gone. The Indians have 'em and you know it! You're just trying to get my share of the diamonds!"

The colonel's suavity disappeared for a moment. "You idiot!" he snarled.

"Listen to me!" Danny cried. "Sergeant! Both these men are crooks. There is a pouch of diamonds in the saddlebags. Cluggage is trying to steal them from his partner, under your eyes! Arrest me if you want to, but you've got to arrest them too!"

At this point there came a bellow from the stagecoach driver, demanding to know why in tarnation he couldn't get started.

"In a minute," the sergeant replied; then he answered

Danny, "I guess the only thing I can do is arrest all of you. I'll take you at least to the next stagecoach station and see what I find out there."

But the two coach passengers now refused to ride inside with the odd assortment of outlaws. In the end the passengers climbed into vacant seats on top of the coach and left the interior entirely to Danny, Cluggage, Teel, and Private Pritchard who sat next to Danny, keeping guard over the lot of them.

The trip down the canyon was sheer torture. Every bounce and bump sent shocks of pain through Danny's battered head. The driver, behind schedule, seemed to feel that the fate of the Republic depended on his making up the lost time. But when the road leveled out a little at the foot of the canyon, the jolts grew fewer, and the swaying of the coach body had a soothing effect. Danny closed his eyes and immediately fell asleep..

A heavy jolt halfway woke him, and he heard a loud snoring on his right. This could only mean that the guard, Private Pritchard, had fallen asleep too. From the opposite seat came angry words that Danny wanted to hear. He kept his eyes tight shut as if he was sound asleep, and he heard the colonel say soothingly, "Don't you see? My proposal that we separate at the pass was the best thing for *you*. They couldn't possibly accuse you of taking the money, and they'd have to release you. As a matter of simple fact, you don't know how or when I got it. That should make it easy for you to keep your story straight."

"You think I'm stupid, don't you?" Teel burst out. "I knew all the time why you didn't go to Jack the Jug's burying. You stayed in the wagon circle so you could pick the lock on the major's strongbox with nobody around to bother you."

"Well, I've got to give you credit!" Cluggage said with a sneer in his voice.

"I let you do too much of the thinking all the way along," Teel went on in an angry undertone. "We should have made our getaway, like I told you, the day the major said he didn't think that the Utes shot my mules. It was the next thing to saying he thought I shot 'em myself. I wish now I hadn't shot them. They were good mules. And that crazy bow and arrow idea of yours that you said would

make it look like a real Indian ambush!"

Again the colonel said in a pacifying tone, "It was just a piece of bad luck that our plans didn't work out. People wouldn't have got suspicious if it hadn't been for that jewel robbery in Santa Fe. In all fairness you'll have to admit that the jewel robbery wasn't my fault any more than it was yours."

"The trouble with you," Teel said bitterly, "is you're never satisfied with a good, cleancut, simple job. You always have to add something fancy to it. It wasn't enough just to have a hatful of diamonds. Oh, no, not for Colonel Valentine Cluggage. He had to use his diamonds to start a whole phony diamond rush in order to sell a bunch of phony stock."

"You stupid oaf!" the colonel snarled. "I was foolish enough to let you choose the place for our mine. You should have known that the Indians get together near there every year for a big powwow. If you didn't know, you should have checked. You had plenty of chance when you were around here prospecting for gold." Suddenly Cluggage paused, and his tone of voice changed again. "See here,

Teel, we're both in this. If we work together we'll come out all right yet. As I see it, there's a perfectly simple solution."

"It's not simple, or you wouldn't think of it. But go ahead."

"There's only one witness against us, right? Now if the boy. . . ."

The voices dropped too low. Danny could not catch the words. Then came silence, except for the creaking and rumbling of the coach and the soldier's snoring.

Danny waited with closed eyes. What did Cluggage have in mind? Danny knew this latest scheme had to do with him, and he was worried. The silence grew more and more frightening, and Danny decided he had better take a peek. He opened one eye a bit. The afternoon sunlight through the coach window fell on something white lying on the seat beyond Private Pritchard. The white something moved. It was a hand—but not Private Pritchard's hand! The fingers pointed the wrong direction. And they were soft and slender. Cluggage was reaching slowly for the sleeping soldier's Colt!

Danny opened the other eye a fraction of an inch.

What he saw made him kick out wildly with both feet at once.

"Wake up! Look out!" he yelled.

19

WANTED!

"It sure was a relief when that soldier woke up," Danny said that night as he stretched out on the ground by the campfire near the major's *Santa Maria*.

"I guess it was a relief to the soldier too," the major added. "In another minute he'd have woke up dead."

"But, Danny," Bizz said in a puzzled voice, "how did you know they were going to kill you again?"

"Well, Cluggage was trying to steal the soldier's revolver, and Teel was standing right over me with his hands ready to choke me if I made any noise. Cluggage was going to shoot the soldier. Then he'd shoot me. He planned to tell everybody that I killed the soldier and that the gun went

273

off accidentally and shot me when he was trying to get it out of my hand."

"Wow-ee!" Bizz said. "Then what?"

"So I kicked Teel in the stomach and Cluggage in the arm, and the soldier woke up."

"Aren't they supposed to shoot soldiers that fall asleep when they're guarding?" Buzz asked.

"Well," Danny said, "I didn't tell on him. And I don't see why Cluggage and Teel would, or why anybody would believe them."

"I think those soldiers that arrested you were stupid," Buzz said emphatically. "Anybody ought to know that Danny doesn't steal."

"I don't know, Bizz," Danny laughed. "The colonel certainly made things look bad for me. Most people in the wagon train believed him when he said I stole the money. He's a good talker. But I guess they know by now that it was his idea to sell them phony mining stock."

"You're right, Danny," said the major. "But, you know, he was so slick that the businessmen in the train thought *they* were having a hard time convincing *him* that he ought to buy stock himself. He was so blooming honest that he wouldn't hold the money. He bamboozled me into holding it, so he would have an easier time stealing it without being suspected. And he fooled me with his scheme for salting the diamonds. I'll never forgive myself for not seeing through that."

"Major," Flint put in, "if wagon trains hadn't been stopped from coming through here because the Utes were having their powwow, Cluggage could have sold stock to every train that passed by here from now until the season ends. Not many trains have as much money along as ours has, but they all have some cash these days. Cluggage would have made a tremendous haul."

"That's the truth. And he could move on next year to some other place, use those same diamonds over and over again—same printing press too."

"But not the same Danny!" said Danny emphatically.

"We know that!" the major assured him.

"I was scared the soldiers really were going to take you to jail in Santa Fe, the way they did the colonel and Mr. Teel," Buzz said.

"I was scared too. And they would have taken me, if it hadn't been for Flint," Danny answered. "I certainly do thank you, Flint, for what you did."

Danny leaned back on an elbow with a sigh. There was no doubt about it, he would be under arrest right now if Flint's sharp eyes hadn't noticed one little thing. Flint had observed that the saddlebags containing the money were the very same saddlebags the colonel had put on his horse this morning. The saddlebags couldn't have been on Tennessee when Danny and the horse both disappeared last night. That meant only one thing: Danny couldn't have left camp with the money, because the saddlebags containing the money were on Cluggage's horse when the colonel rode off from the wagon circle many hours later.

"Major," Danny said, "there's one thing I haven't been able to figure out. Why did Teel pick this particular place for his phony diamond mine?"

"I know the answer to that one," Flint said. "I talked to a fellow at the stagecoach station up the line today. He said Teel was a sure-enough prospector—came through here last summer looking for gold. Teel was telling the truth when he said he panned for it up this stream."

"It still doesn't explain why he thought that gravel bed was a good place to salt with diamonds."

"It was a little like the kind of place where the papers say they have been finding diamonds in Africa," the major answered. "And it was an easy place for him to salt, real persuasive-like. He got me to dig just where he wanted me to dig, and all of the time I thought I was picking the spot for myself."

Danny had to smile. The major being apologetic!

"What beats me is how a fellow could scatter real diamonds around the way Cluggage and Teel did," the major went on. "Those things are worth a lot of money. I just wonder where Cluggage got 'em."

"Don't you know?" Bizz said wonderingly. "I thought everybody knew and that was why they arrested him. It was all written out on that piece of paper."

"What piece of paper, Bizz?" Flint asked.

"The one Caleb found."

"Where is it?" Danny asked eagerly. "What did you do with it after you looked at it?"

"I don't know," Buzz answered. "We just put it somewhere."

"Well, go find it!" Danny ordered.

Reluctantly, protesting they didn't see why they should bother, the two went off. Presently they returned with a crumpled sheet of paper.

" 'Wanted,' " Danny read. "What do you know! It's a handbill. I've set up lots of 'em myself, but I never saw one from Africa before!"

"What's this?" the major interrupted.

"It says they want to find a fellow who says he's an American and goes by the name of Colonel Valentine Cluggage. Seems he was over in Africa in the big diamond rush and he stole a whole mess of diamonds from a man who dug 'em out of a mine!"

"Where do you suppose Caleb found that handbill?" Flint wondered.

"I don't suppose—I know," Bizz answered. "He took it out of the secret hiding place in the colonel's wagon. I saw him."

"But why in the world would Cluggage carry this around

with him? This would just make trouble for him if anybody found it."

The major answered thoughtfully, "I guess he figured he was so much smarter than anybody else that he could afford a little joke like that. It tickled his vanity to carry around proof that he'd got away with a fortune in diamonds. I guess he must have been a wee mite excited when he cleared out of here this morning, or he would have remembered to take it with him."

The major paused. "Speaking of clearing out of here," he said, "we have to be on the road bright and early. When the twin chiefs were here this afternoon, they as much as said I was a heap of stir and no biscuits. But I gave 'em my word that nothing was going to hold me back this time. And nothing is. By the way, Danny, the Utes seem to think you're a pretty fine fellow."

"Wouldn't *you* like me if I gave you two mighty fine horses and saddles?"

"You have a point, but I got the impression there's more to it than that. Anyway, that's enough talk for now. Let's turn in. Tomorrow we start early. A coyote that sleeps late doesn't have rabbit for breakfast, I always say. Tomorrow we want to be in good shape when we pass that wagon train that sneaked by us in the storm the other side of Trinidad."

"Are you fixing to fly, Major?" Flint asked. "That train must be a good three days ahead of us by now."

"They *were* three days ahead, you mean. But it's funny how word about a thing like diamonds can get spread around."

"Major! You don't really mean you spread word around —sent word ahead?" Flint asked.

Danny was shocked. "But that would encourage men in that train to come back here where the Utes will probably kill them!"

"I didn't say they were coming back here. Flint, you know that old cinder cone we have to pass tomorrow morning on the left-hand side of the trail?"

"Yeah."

"Did you ever hear any legends about it?"

"I only know the Utes think it's bad medicine for some reason. They won't go within a mile of it."

"Uh-huh. Well, sir, I bet you we find everybody in that wagon train is up there on that cinder cone looking for diamonds tomorrow morning, while we sail right on past. And, Flint, I want you to do me a favor. I want you to ride over and show the captain of the train this handbill. I surely hate to see anybody waste time digging diamonds where there ain't any."

Flint grinned. "It'll be a pleasure." Chuckling, he left the fire and went off to roll up in his buffalo robe.

Danny spread his own robe under the *Poor Richard*.

From a perch on the front axle of the wagon came a greeting:

"Hi, Danny."

"Hi, Caleb."

"Holy Moses!"